DEMON SWORN

THE CAMELOT ARCHIVE - BOOK TWO

NICOLE R. TAYLOR

1

___

L ondon was busier than I remembered.

I'd been at Camelot for a month, but it felt like an eternity after everything I'd been through. The city was crowded, buildings pressed in on me, and it was full of pollution. After spending my whole life dreaming of being stationed here after my training, it was ironic that I was longing for the countryside. Stillness and stars were foreign concepts here.

I sat inside the London Sanctum, the headquarters of the Naturals—the demon-hunting mages who protected the Earth from the Darkness beyond—awaiting the ultimate question time.

The hall was empty, though I could hear the murmuring of voices through the carved double doors in front of me—and they didn't sound happy.

I shuffled my boots over the marble floor tiles, studying the pattern of black and grey as it splintered through white stone. Anything to keep my mind focused.

In the last month, I'd broken just about every rule, regulation, and covenant laid out in the Codex. The humans had their various religions with their sacred texts, and the Naturals had theirs in the Codex. No one was exempt from a higher power, though we knew for sure ours existed. The Lady of the Lake, a celestial being of unknown origins who'd gifted the first Naturals with their power and had given us Excalibur and Arondight.

"Madeleine Greenbriar."

My heart leapt and I looked up to find a familiar face staring down at me. A tall, gangly man with messy brown hair and a rumpled T-shirt with the slogan 'keep calm and respawn' on the front grinned down at me. I assumed the writing on the shirt was a video game reference—he was a professional gamer before joining the Sanctum—but it went straight over my head.

"Jackson?"

"Hey," he replied and sat beside me. "I can't say I'm surprised, but that's a nice jacket. It goes especially well with the combat boots."

"Still hilarious, I see."

He grinned and leaned against the wall. Jackson was the human best friend of Arondight—otherwise known as Scarlett Ravenwood—and had once been like me. As a victim of Human Convergence, he was mutated with demonic genes through possession. He'd been cured after the death of Mordred—the twisted Natural the Dark had synthesised the infection from—and was now one hundred percent human.

"How's Esme?" Esme was his wife and fellow Human Convergence survivor.

"Great," he replied. "She's heading up the infirmary while Ramona is at Camelot."

"And how are your inventions coming along? Built anything yet?"

"I'm working on a device to detect demonic possession," he told me. "It's to do with particle waves and quantum physics. I know you're supposed to be able to do that stuff now, but we're not as lucky."

"I didn't ask for this, you know."

He frowned. "Yeah, I know. I don't think anyone saw this coming when Scarlett saved your soul."

"I'm glad she did, though. Being wiped from existence would have sucked."

Jackson nodded towards the assembly. "What are you going to tell them?"

That was the question of the day. The enemy had captured me, I'd been imprisoned by my own people —twice—escaped both times, constantly defied orders, and teamed up with a demon to save Camelot. Most of those things were punishable by exile, even with the stripping of Light—the power that made a Natural who they were—but I wasn't exactly the same person I was when I'd been demoted to guard duty at the archeological site of Camelot.

The greater demon, Ikakantor, had awoken the dormant demonic mutation lodged in my soul, intending to use me to uncover some secret buried below the castle. After being forced to accept who I was becoming to save my friends, I was now half Light and half Dark.

And what that meant exactly was anyone's guess, least of all mine.

Then there was Elijah…

"I don't know," I said, finally replying to Jackson's question.

"The truth always helps," he commented as he glanced past me. "What happened to Wilder wasn't your fault."

Following his gaze, I noted the guards stationed at the end of the hall. Looking in the other direction, two more men stood by the double doors leading out to the main foyer of the Sanctum.

They trusted me…to a point. It wouldn't take any effort for me to walk out of here. I wouldn't even have to raise a hand. Being a part of both worlds, I could nullify the powers of both. I hadn't tried the Dark yet and had failed miserably when I'd tried, but I understood Light and getting past it was easy. Training your whole life to become a warrior was good for times like these, though it was terrible for building trust.

"Madeleine."

I looked up at the Natural down the hall. The tall man I didn't recognise was a representative from the Regula, the governing body of the Naturals.

"They're ready for you."

I nodded and rose to my feet, smoothing down my black suit jacket. First impressions counted, especially when you were accused of consorting with the enemy.

"Good luck," Jackson said, rising with me. "Remember—"

"Jackson." I pouted and brushed him off.

"I know, but my fickle human heart wants to say it out loud."

I attempted a smile, but I was entirely positive it looked like a twisted grimace. Turning towards the doors, I pushed them open and strode inside. Better to get this over and done with as soon as possible.

The gallery was a large round room with a domed skylight. Tiered seating surrounded the entire space, climbing five levels. Eight hundred Naturals could cram themselves in here, but only one hundred were stationed in London at any one time. They weren't all warriors, but support personnel like scientists, doctors, cooks, trainers, researchers, and assistants. Of that number, less than half patrolled the city, protecting its people against demonic possession.

I supposed that's why everyone took things so seriously around here. The loss of one was the loss of many.

I stood in the centre of the gallery, illuminated in a circle of overcast light filtering through the dome, and looked up at the representatives sent by the Regula. Wilder was the Inquisitor—the Naturals' version of a Prime Minister—but ever since he'd fallen into a coma—which was another reason I was here—Greer had taken his place.

Greer was the protector of the Codex. Selected by fate and powers beyond reasoning, she alone was tasked with keeping the powerful book safe, recounting its lessons and adding new pages. If an unworthy touched it, they'd burn from the inside out. It was one hell of a firewall, *pun intended.*

She could be sweet with her angelic face, blemish free skin, shiny almond-coloured hair, and perfect wardrobe, but her wrath was terrible.

To her right sat Aldrich, Scarlett's uncle and long-time council member at the London Sanctum. He now served as part of the Regula beside the Inquisitor. Grey-haired and weathered by decades fighting on the front lines, he was wise, calm, and the fatherly figure everyone wish they had.

To her left was a man I didn't recognise and to my annoyance, no one bothered to introduce him. He looked a little young to be sitting beside such esteemed Naturals, but I wasn't in the position to question the authority of our government. They assured me I wasn't on trial, but it sure felt like it.

I could tell the new guy was handsome, but he wasn't my type. He was clean cut and impeccably dressed in a tailored black suit jacket and crisp navy shirt. His sharp green eyes stared at me like I was transparent. His caramel-coloured hair even had that artful swoosh that was meticulously styled to look like he rolled out of bed that way. Even so, I wasn't blind. He was good-looking, but I usually went for men with darker colouring and who were a little rugged around the edges—like Elijah.

My heart twisted at the thought of him. The last time I'd seen the half-demon, he'd given in to his Dark side, cut Ikakantor's head off to save Camelot, then told me to take all the credit so I could keep my place amongst the Naturals. Who knew where he was now?

"Madeleine Greenbriar, you stand here accused of treason, assault, and conspiracy," Greer said, her voice echoing through the chamber. "Among other things."

"You conspired to flee with a demon," Aldrich said. "Why?"

I cleared my throat. "He freed me from a greater demon's lair. In exchange, all he wanted was help with finding a cure—"

"A cure you couldn't give," the unknown man stated. He even sounded posh.

"No, but—"

"And why was that?" he pressed, cutting me off yet again.

"Because Ramona found he wasn't mutated like I had been. He was different."

"Different how?" Greer asked.

"She never got the time to find that out," I replied.

"Because you broke out of your bonds and helped him escape," the man snapped.

"I left because no one believed my intentions or Elijah's were good," I said, my voice rising. "You're all too hung up on the fact that I have some bad guy's DNA to see the threat growing on our doorstep. If I hadn't broken out and stopped Ikakantor, the Dark would have used the Naturals to finish digging up

Camelot and this conversation we're having would be very different."

"What is the Dark looking for?" he demanded.

I rolled my eyes. "How would I know?"

"You're connected to the Dark. You tell me."

"Careful," I hissed, "your prejudice is showing."

"Enough," Greer snapped, slamming her fist down onto the table.

"Madeleine, you obviously have some strong opinions," Aldrich urged, his voice a welcome calm amongst the rising tension. "Tell us what you would do."

"You shouldn't be so hung up on following the law as it was written in an eight hundred-year-old book," I told them. "The Codex was created in a world under threat from the demonic creatures beyond the rift. Now the rift is closed and the Dark which remains isn't the same enemy. The Light must evolve just as the Dark has or it will perish. The future is here, and it is in jeopardy. We can't rely on archaic beliefs to save the world from an evolving threat."

"They'd be wise words if they weren't coming from a hybrid," the man spat. "A hybrid who can nullify Light and do whatever the hell she wants."

"*Issac*," Greer snapped, "we do not judge with hostility within these walls."

"She said it herself," the man known as Issac argued. "We can't rely on *archaic beliefs*."

"There is a shred of truth in her words," Aldrich said. "It is folly to remain still when the enemy is speeding up."

"Perhaps," Issac shook his head, "but she accepted her soul and merged her powers the same night a greater demon attacked Camelot and the Twin Flames fell into a coma."

"Scarlett was nowhere near Camelot," Aldrich told him.

"It doesn't matter," Issac countered. "The Twin Flames are linked. If one falls, they both suffer."

My heart plummeted. "Scarlett's sick?" *Why didn't Jackson tell me?*

Greer sighed and nodded. "Whatever ailment has taken Wilder has also affected Scarlett."

"Where is she? Can I—"

Issac snorted. "Do you really think we would let you anywhere near the Flames?"

"She saved my life!" I exclaimed, my voice echoing around the gallery. "Why would I wish this on her?"

"Because when she saved your life, your soul came back along with the Darkness that infected you," Issac told me. "It isn't beyond reason you'd harbour ill will towards her for that."

"No! You're putting words in my mouth."

Greer rose to her feet, cutting Issac off. "*Enough.*" Her gaze found mine and I thought I saw a shred of pity in them. "You slew Ikakantor and broke his hold over the Naturals at Camelot," she continued. "However, you attacked a fellow Natural, escaped confinement not once but twice, and conspired to free a demon who is now unaccounted for. Do you deny it?"

I jutted out my chin. "No, I do not."

"Where is the demon Elijah?" she pressed.

"Hybrid," I corrected. "He was mutated. Ramona has the evidence."

She nodded, her lips thin. "Where is the hybrid?"

"I don't know."

"Convenient," Issac spat.

"He left after I slew Ikakantor's body, fearing he'd be cut open and experimented on," I said, seething. "And I don't blame him. I will make it a point that if it wasn't for Elijah, we wouldn't know the Balan demon's true name."

"She's sympathetic to them," Issac hissed at the others. "What's stopping her from turning against us? If she goes Dark, we can't do anything."

Greer turned to face him, her eyes narrowing. "You," she said evenly. "You're stopping her."

"Excuse me?" he and I blurted it at the same time, looking at each other with open dislike.

"It's clear your newfound abilities require further study," she went on. "And that they are linked to your emotions. I do not doubt your intentions, Madeleine, but we all understand how emotions can get the better of us. We do have a human element to our species, after all."

"You believe me?" I asked, my mouth falling open.

"I believe you had no part in the sickness that overcame Wilder. Aiden Thompson mentioned the vault in Camelot's archive was emitting a strange power that may have something to do with it, and the timing was within range. *However...* more study is needed and my benevolence towards your multiple insurrections comes with certain conditions."

I nodded, lowering my gaze. It was wishful thinking to hope that I'd walk out of here without some kind of punishment, but at least Greer seemed to be leaning towards not throwing me into prison in the Glastonbury catacombs. That place was dark, wet, and miserable.

"You will return to Camelot and assist Aiden with the cataloging of the archive. Your abilities may be a welcome benefit for his continued studies. This was his request, so do not disappoint him a third time. While not in his service, you will report to Issac once daily for training. He will assist you with controlling and developing your abilities."

"Impossible," he complained.

Greer turned her glare onto Issac. "This is not negotiable. It's a direct order, Issac." To me, she added yet another condition, "You must understand your new reality, Madeleine, and earn the Naturals' trust back."

"The Naturals?" I narrowed my eyes. "So, I'm no longer seen as one of you?"

She didn't honour me with a response, just the ultimate full stop. "And you must inform us immediately if the demon-hybrid Elijah contacts you, otherwise we will have no choice but to confine you. Am I clear?"

My jaw tightened and I stood tall. There was no way I was going to let Issac see a single shred of weakness in me. He was determined to see me fail, I was sure of it.

"Yes," I said, "I understand."

"Then you will return to Camelot this evening." Greer nodded and gestured towards the doors. "Dismissed."

I shot Issac one last glare, salty over the fact that I'd have to share a car with him for the three hours back to base camp. Cataloguing dusty scrolls and pottery, and daily training with the ultimate prejudiced arsehole was going to wear thin, real quick. I wasn't born yesterday.

I'd just been given a babysitter.

2

The Sanctum was empty as I strode through the halls, the once familiar building cold.

Even with the Regula in session, the Naturals were spread thin across the city. We were few before the rift closed, and afterwards…many had been lost. It would take decades to recover, if we ever did.

There I went saying 'we' again. My scowl deepened as I recalled the look on Greer's face. *So, I'm no longer seen as one of you?*

I wanted to go see Esme and Jackson before I left, but I was hesitant. Everyone had always looked at me differently, but now that I'd turned into something else, even those who'd been on my side had taken a step back.

I was the only one of my kind. Isolated, distrusted…and now I had a babysitter who hated my guts. Could this life get any better?

Instead, I went to the gallery where I could be alone. It was my last chance to stand on my own without being watched, where I didn't have to hide my emotions or watch my back. Maybe these feelings were why I liked the quiet of Camelot.

My boots squeaked against the polished floorboards as I passed portraits of famous Naturals, battle scenes, and landscapes. Where war and suffering took hold, the Dark lingered…and the Light was there to eradicate it. Revolutions, World Wars, political coups, nuclear stand offs—it was all there on the walls.

Many of the paintings had been saved and restored after the Dark Night—when Mordred had led a coordinated attack on the Sanctums across the world—and now they hung in the new gallery. I was told it looked much like the old one, but I'd never had the chance to see it. I'd spent most of my time here in the infirmary before graduating.

It was only after I'd become a fully-fledged Natural that I'd been able to see the paintings which depicted our modern history.

Was I able to still call myself a Natural? Elijah had given me the name of spectre—a ghost who walked in both worlds, neither Light nor Dark.

I studied the portrait in front of me, my gaze following the brush strokes and how the colours mixed together. It was an iridescent rendering of the Lady of the Lake. Who she was, where she came from, and what her true name was…all of it was a mystery. She'd remained in Avalon, sealing off the pocket of space and time from our world after she'd awoken

Scarlett as Arondight. Now, we'd never know the truth of her identity, but I wondered if that was for the best.

A cough echoed behind me and I turned with a scowl. Issac stood by the painting of Elizabeth Clare, the warrior who'd wielded my arondight blade before me—the same arondight blade that had been permanently confiscated from me. I resented him for sharing the same space as one of my idols, even though it was only a painting of her.

Now that he was standing, I could see he was quite tall. He stood almost a head over me and I wasn't short by any means. I decided his fancy suit and hipster hairstyle made him look pompous.

Issac felt no kindness towards me, let alone any indifference. I was an annoyance they forced him to deal with. Strange how my opinion mirrored his.

"We will be leaving for Camelot in one hour," he said almost robotically.

"Great. Can't wait."

We stared one another down for a long minute before he said, "I don't like this any more than you do, but orders are orders."

"What qualifies *you* to train *me*?" I asked, not bothering to mask my vehement dislike of the guy.

"I specialise in the development of Light technologies," he stated, his lip curling. "Otherwise known as the evolution you so dearly believe in."

"Fancy," I drawled.

"It's more important than wading through rotting corpses on the street." If that was his attempt at insulting my career choice then he totally missed the mark.

"I bet you thought you'd hit the jackpot when Greer asked you to sit on the Regula for an extra special hearing, didn't you?" I laughed and shook my head. "Now you just get to work with the dirty demon girl in the slush of a ruined city. Who did you piss off?"

Issac narrowed his eyes. "Make it fifty minutes to departure. Don't be late, Madeline…you can't afford another mark against your name." He raked his gaze over me, his expression giving nothing away, then left.

I scowled and glared after him. Who did this guy think he was? The Lord of the Lake?

I shook my head and glanced at the painting of Elizabeth Clare. She'd been in Paris during the French Revolution and had famously gone undercover with a demonic cult to root out a greater demon. I wondered what she'd make of me.

It didn't matter. I was half Dark, but I was still half Light, no matter what Issac or anyone else said. His hatred would not get to me.

I'd made a vow to Aiden, Ramona, Scarlett, and Wilder. A vow to earn back their trust and find a cure for the sickness that had sent the Twin Flames into a coma.

And I intended to keep it.

Issac wasn't lying when he said he wanted to leave on time.

I was practically shoved headfirst into a black sedan in the undercover garage. Luckily, I only had a small duffle bag—full of new issue uniforms—because that flew in behind me.

Thankfully, he took the front seat beside the driver, so I sat in the back and imagined my glare was burning a hole into his skull. He never looked back or uttered a word to me, so at least shooting laser beams out of my eyes wasn't an ability I could add to the list. One assault charge on my record was more than enough.

After three hours of awkward silence, Camelot finally came into view. Returning, even after a few days, was bittersweet. I'd saved everyone from Ikakantor's thrall, but it had done nothing to calm the hostility towards me. Dealing with it was my new reality and I wasn't sure it would ever change—no matter how many heroic deeds I accomplished.

Night had fallen while we were on the road. Summer was long over and autumn was fading. Winter in the city was going to be a muddy and freezing affair.

The castle and its lower city covered several hundred hectares of overgrown and crumbling stone buildings. That included the castle with its inner bailey, service buildings, and gardens. Then the upper city, full of posh people and their fancy villas, then the lower tiers where the common folk went about their business.

It always awed me how so many people had lived here during the Middle Ages, only to succumb to the incursion of the Dark during the cataclysm. The Naturals had lost so much. Not only scores of people, but the history and knowledge that made them so powerful.

The car passed through the veil concealing the city from the outside world, and I looked out the window at the ruined city that had caused so much chaos in my life. The night shrouded most of the ruins in shadow, but the artificial lights illuminating the base camp shimmered through the illusion like a beacon.

Time and space were folded here, meaning the city within was much larger than the outside world had believed. If a human stumbled across it on a hike, they'd walk through an illusion that spat them out on the other side, none the wiser for what lay just beyond their reach.

Whoever had placed the wards around this place was unknown, but it must have taken considerable power to cover hundreds of hectares and to last almost a thousand years.

Druids, I thought. *Had to be.* But they were gone, the last passing through the Darklands to reach their homeland in the years following the cataclysm. Gone, just like Elijah.

I wondered if I was right about him—if he'd been a Druid before he was mutated. I didn't know, he'd always been tight-lipped about his origins. Either way, I'd keep my suspicions to myself.

The car bumped up the dirt track, the uneven surface wreaking havoc on the suspension. At the top of the rise, we stopped at a checkpoint which was a new addition. Security had been beefed up to extreme since I'd been in London. The Regula weren't taking any chances.

A Natural dressed head to toe in tactical gear leaned down and peered into the car. I spotted his arondight blade at his hip, the silver hilt glinting in the light from the tent behind him.

Issac rolled down his window and gestured for the man to come to the passenger side.

"Identification, please," the Natural said, angling his head so he could look at me.

Issac handed him some papers and the Natural took his sweet time checking over everything. His brow creased and he looked at me again.

"Thank you, Mr. Worthington," he said, handing back the papers. "Thompson is awaiting your arrival in the command tent. Vehicles can be left in the space to the right. Welcome to Camelot."

I snorted as Issac rolled the window back up and the driver accelerated through the checkpoint. Someone took their job a little too seriously. Camelot was far from customs and immigration.

The driver parked the car as directed and I climbed out of the back, dragging my duffle bag with me.

Issac walked through the mud as if he didn't have a care in the world. His boots squelched, his posh woollen overcoat out of place amongst the ruined walls of Camelot, though he strode through the camp like he owned it.

Nothing had changed since I'd been away. Apart from the increased security around the perimeter, everything looked exactly the same. After only a few days, I wasn't sure what I was expecting. Armoured tanks, perhaps? An enormous, rumbling machine wasn't exactly the first choice for a secret organisation.

We went straight to the command tent.

Thompson looked at me like I was a problem he didn't need, though I couldn't blame him. I'd walked through his Light barrier like it was nothing. That had to dent his fragile manly pride.

"Worthington," he said, holding out his hand, "right on time."

Issac shook his proffered hand and looked around the tent. "Still messy, I see."

I stood to the side, watching their exchanged like a hawk. *Great. They were friends.*

"I was surprised when the Regula said they were sending you," Thompson said.

"So was I." They glanced at me and I curled my lip.

"I'm honoured to be granted the babysitting services of such an esteemed Natural," I declared.

"Don't mind Madeleine," Thompson said, glaring at me. "She's always like that."

"One would hope that the attitude is linked to her demonic mutation," Issac said like I wasn't standing there. "But there is also wishful thinking."

Thompson snorted and swallowed a laugh.

"It's not a mutation." They fell silent and looked at me.

Issac cleared his throat and turned to face me. "Tomorrow you will report for training at dawn."

"Dawn?" I complained.

"*Dawn*," Issac said, casting me a withering look. "After which you are permitted to eat in the mess tent. Then you are to report to Aiden Thompson at the archive."

"You're so cheery," I told him. "The life of the party."

"I don't need to remind you that you are here because of the Regula's benevolence. What has been given can be taken away."

I pouted and my shoulders sagged. Consider me pushed back into my hole.

"Where?" I asked.

"My tent…" He glanced at Thompson.

"The other side of the camp. D3," the commander replied, giving out the address.

I raised an eyebrow. "And me?"

"You will resume your previous lodgings in the barracks," Thompson said.

I wasn't born yesterday. What better way to make sure I was monitored at all times than to throw me back into the snake pit.

I should count myself lucky. At least it wasn't that windowless stone room they locked me in last time.

"You are dismissed," Issac said, turning his back on me.

I didn't think I could feel any more like an

outsider, but in that moment, my position was clear. Madeleine Greenbriar was a liability, an annoyance, and a burden no one wanted. They were going all out to make sure my soul didn't align with the Dark.

Leaving the command tent, I stepped out into the night. I cast my gaze over the base camp and just to spite Thompson and Issac, I willed myself into invisibility—a skill I'd mastered fairly quickly.

Crossing the camp, I pressed the edges of my unknown powers, testing the limits of my concealment. Who knew what else I could do, but I supposed I'd find that answer out tomorrow at dawn.

I stepped into the barracks, my duffle slung over my shoulder, and looked around. Several Naturals glanced up at my arrival, verifying that I'd phased back into view. There wasn't a sympathetic face amongst the bunch, and I bristled.

So that was the thanks I got for saving Camelot from Ikakantor's thrall. Good to know.

Rhys rose to his feet, his dislike clear from the sour look that puckered his lips. The last time I'd seen him was when my fist had collided with his ugly face, and the feeling was mutual. He had tried to incite a lynch mob against me, so in my book, I was totally justified in breaking his nose. Unfortunately, my book wasn't the Codex.

"Look who's back," he snarled. "The demon walks amongst us."

A thank you might have been nice, but who was I kidding? I should have left his nasty arse in that demonic thrall, but that was the thing about having a conscious… A guy like Rhys would never understand sacrifice.

I sighed. Arguing was futile.

"She thinks she saved us, but who's saying it wasn't a plot with the Dark to win back our trust?"

Turning, I left the barracks. There was no way I was sleeping there. I'd probably never wake up if I did.

It was a bittersweet return to Camelot.

I wandered through the camp, passing a few open tents as I went. A scientist was hunched over a microscope in one, and a researcher cleaning dirt and clay off a large round amphora with a tiny brush was inside another.

And so, life went on.

I dumped my bag beside the bonfire in the centre of the miniature tent city and sat on a stool. Staring into the flames, depression began to take hold.

Why did I come back to Camelot? Maybe I should have gone with Elijah, even though he'd given himself to his demon side to save me from Ikakantor. He knew things about what I was changing into, and even though he'd annoy me with his terrible insults more than anything, I'd be happier.

But I couldn't just run away from my problems. Scarlett and Wilder were sick, and the Dark was attempting to rise again. Another war might erupt, and my powers bridged the gap between both sides.

I was doing this to protect life, just like the Naturals were, but I wasn't doing it in the name of the Light. I chose neither Light nor Dark—I'd chosen life.

I'd told Elijah I'd do whatever it took to make sure the Dark didn't get their hands on whatever they wanted in Camelot, but I didn't realise it was going to be this hard.

I was back at square one. Actually, I was less than that. Instead of making things better, they'd gotten worse.

I glanced at the sky and shivered. It was going to be a cold night under the stars. I tapped into my Light—the power I still held as half-Natural—and allowed it to warm my blood. At least some things were still the same.

3

———

Dawn was a strange time in Camelot.

Patrols were changing over, people were waking up, and the sound of Naturals training in the yard echoed across the camp. More personnel had arrived in my absence, so when I woke up by the bonfire, I had an audience.

I sat up, my back stiff from the hard ground, and ignored the startled looks and amused sniggers.

Gathering my things, I dragged myself over to Issac's tent to report for training. Whatever that entailed…

The tent flap opened as I arrived and Issac appeared, perfectly put together as usual.

"You look terrible," he said, going straight for flattery. "Are the barracks that bad?"

"I'm not sleeping in the barracks."

He sighed. "Where *did* you sleep?"

"On the ground by the bonfire."

"Yes, now that you mention it, I can smell that." Issac wrinkled his nose. "Why on earth—" He stopped himself and shook his head.

"You do you, and I'll do me," I told him. "I'm here to learn about my abilities, so let's just do that and skip all the judgemental small talk."

He stared at me for a moment, then said, "Leave your bag at the door and come in."

I hesitated. I wasn't sure what to expect, but I'd had visions of training in the yard or a secluded part of the city away from prying eyes. Anything but inside Issac's tent.

"We're training here?" I asked.

"This isn't fight training, Madeleine." He held the tent flap open. "Leave your bag by the door and come inside."

Issac looked thoroughly annoyed at having to repeat himself, so I did as he commanded. It wasn't the fact that we were training in a tent, rather that it was his space.

There wasn't much to see inside. We'd only arrived last night, so personalisation hadn't happened yet and it put me at ease. I didn't want to know anything about Issac Worthington.

I was jealous of his double bed. It was little more than a foldable camp bed with a basic mattress, blankets, and pillows, but it beat the ground and those lumpy bunks in the barracks. At the thought of the hostile welcome I'd received last night, I wondered where I'd find some peace tonight.

There wasn't much else in the tent besides basic amenities. A metal trunk sat at the foot of the bed and a small table to one side with a matching chair where Issac's fancy overcoat lay folded over the back. Other than a plain beige woven mat on the ground, the rest of the space was empty.

I stood to the side as Issac picked up the pillows and set them on the mat. Watching him closely, I wondered what his 'training' would entail. There was no way I was holding his hands and singing campfire songs.

He sat cross-legged on one pillow and gestured for me to do the same.

"What is this?" I asked, glancing at the innocent cushion as if it was booby-trapped.

"Sit down, Madeleine."

I tensed and did as he said. It wasn't like I had a choice. Greer had commanded we work together, and she was the Inquisitor in Wilder's absence.

Crossing my legs, I straightened my back and waited.

Issac held out his hands.

Just the thing I didn't want to do. Touching was bad—even the youngest Natural understood how easy it was to connect with someone else's power that way. "What are you doing?"

"Take my hands," he prompted.

He was opening himself up to me. Even without my Dark side, it would still have been enough for my Light to latch onto his, but this? It was far too dangerous for a guy who claimed to hate me. It was a test, it had to be.

"You're taking a real risk here," I told him slowly. "I thought you didn't trust me."

"Madeleine, you can leave Camelot at any time you choose, and we both know that no one could stop you. That's if they even saw you in the first place. If you're serious about your intentions to help us find a cure for the Flames and fight against Ikakantor, then you won't screw it up—despite your obvious dislike of me."

"I—"

"Do you want to understand and control what you've become, or not?"

I grasped his hands and gritted my teeth. "Yes, sir."

Warmth brushed against my power as his Light reached out towards me. I recoiled, unsure of his intentions.

"Don't withdraw," he said, tightening his grip. "I need to know what we're dealing with."

I drew in a deep breath and let down my barriers—not an easy feat when the guy sitting across from me harboured a grudge the size of the rift.

"Close your eyes."

I did as he said and hoped he liked disappointment as I let my power react to his. My tight control over the unknown loosened and I fell into a strange dream state. I'd been here before, having done these exercises in Light Studies at the

Academy, but as the darkness cleared, the vision that appeared was not my own.

I was in Issac's head.

I almost pulled back, but remembering his order, I let the image solidify. There wasn't much to it anyway.

I was in a library. One of the old-fashioned kind with tall shelves and thousands of hardcover books. The table I sat at was stained in a rich cherry hue with a red leather inset to protect the surface. A notebook was open in front of me, the lined paper covered with scrawled notes. The handwriting wasn't mine, but someone had passionate handwriting, that's for sure. Beside it, was a textbook.

"Worthington."

I tensed at the sound of Issac's name. I wasn't just in his head, I was living his memory in first person. *Great, just great.*

Issac didn't react, though I felt this heartbeat speed up.

"I'm talking to you," the male voice snapped. He had a broad American accent and the sound of it was unfamiliar.

"I've got nothing to say to you," Issac replied.

The unknown male fisted his hand into Issac's hair. "Nothing gives you the right to mess with me, you hear?"

As if to punctuate his point, he slammed Issac's head down onto the table.

"Keep your nose out of other people's business," the bully snarled, "or next time I'll hit harder."

Issac wiped at the blood dripping out of his nose

and held onto his anger. Drops of red fell onto the notebook and seeped into the fibres. He was two years ahead. He was smarter than this. *Stronger.*

He stood and turned towards the unknown male. If the Natural Academy in America had a version of football jocks, then this guy was it. His broad shoulders and muscles were enough to deter Issac alone, but then the guy stood a foot taller than him.

"You got something to say, Worthington?" The bully laughed. "Try it."

Issac shook his head and slammed his fist into the guy's stomach. With a touch of Light behind it, the blow made the bully double over. While he was down, Issac shoved his shoulder and heaved.

The unknown arsehole flew backwards into a table, the crash—

Issac tore his hands from mine, jerking me back into the present. The tent waved back into my line of vision as did his annoyingly perfect face.

"It seems I was correct," he muttered, glaring at me.

"Don't look at me like that," I snapped. "You said you were sure. Oh, and FYI, I didn't want to know anything about you."

"I was sure, but that's not what concerns me."

"You invited me in," I argued.

"Only a little."

I didn't understand. I looked him over, trying to puzzle out what he meant. He was trying to trick me into using more of my Dark side. "You think I can do everything a demon can, don't you? That's insane."

"Delve into memories—"

"That's nothing new. Naturals can do that."

"When Ikakantor subjected you to torture, what did he do?"

"He…" I frowned and shook my head. "He forced me to relive a traumatic experience, but—"

"He manipulated it," Issac stated. "Greater demons can change memories to suit their own ends, Madeleine."

"And you're saying I can do that, too?"

He snorted. "You just did."

"No, I—" I closed my mouth and looked away, my skin crawling. I felt dirty. Delving into a stranger's private memories was one thing, but changing them? It was an accident, but it was a gross violation. "You never fought back, did you?"

"No." He shook his head. "You are made up of Light and Dark. And with it, comes everything that they are."

"Everything? At this rate, I'll never earn my freedom back," I said, my blood pressure rising. "Next you'll tell me I can possess people and command lesser demons!" He stared at me unamused. "Don't look at me like that!"

"It's not outside the realm of possibility."

"I'm not one of them," I hissed, rising to my feet. "I won't let you twist this, Issac. I won't let you incriminate me over something I can't control. I didn't ask for this."

Issac stood and grasped my shoulders. "Calm down," he murmured, showing me a shred of kindness that startled me into silence. "You've been given terrible power, Madeleine. Power that can consume and corrupt even the purest of hearts. That's why I'm here. To ensure that that doesn't happen."

"You're doing one hell of a job," I drawled. "If you look outside, I'm sure you'll see a bunch of demonstrators with signs with witty slogans about how I'll be the death of everyone and everything."

"You're letting your emotions rule you, Madeline," Issac said. "Don't."

"That's easy for you to say! You're just as hateful as they are, or have you forgotten the things you said to me at the hearing?"

Issac's expression turned cold. "I have my orders and so do you. I suggest you abide by them."

And there it was. I shoved his hands away and swallowed my pride. I'd lost my cool, *again*, when I'd vowed not to.

"I can change memories and nullify the strongest Light," I said. "How am I supposed to show you I can be trusted when you know I can turn myself into the ultimate weapon no one can stop? I lose no matter what I do."

"You begin by not using your abilities," he said. "The threat of what you're capable of is why everyone is so afraid."

"You want me to hide?"

"Restraint is the smartest thing you can do," he replied.

"How old are you anyway? You don't look a day over nappies."

His lips quirked. "I thought we were skipping the judgemental small talk."

I lowered my gaze, my cheeks heating. It was embarrassing, knowing he could see the colour deepening. *Damn being so pale.* "I feel like a pawn in a game I don't understand. What's stopping you from telling everyone what I can do?"

"What we do here is confidential," he assured me. "Other than my reports to Greer, no one else has authorisation."

Great. Red tape was the only thing protecting me from being tied to a stake.

"You're young, Madeline," he murmured. "Youth blinds us from responsibilities and consequences. One day you'll look back and see how you should have done things differently. If we didn't have our abilities, then perhaps we'd have the freedom to enjoy this time in our lives. Our goal is to grow as much as we can to serve a higher purpose. Not for glory, but for the greater good. The world at large will never know what we've done for them, and perhaps even those amongst us won't, either. Sacrifice without a thought for oneself is the ultimate gift."

I narrowed my eyes and allowed his words to percolate like coffee beans in my head. Elijah and I had saved Camelot from Ikakantor, but no one would ever know his contribution. What he'd done for us—despite the hate he faced—was a true sacrifice. I could argue the same where Rhys and my special band of haters were concerned—I'd returned to Camelot despite the welcome I'd receive.

But I couldn't help but wonder, was I growing fast enough?

My first training session with Issac had left me bruised and battered. Home truths stuck in my heart like barbed arrowheads and I breathed deeply. That was another thing he'd shown me—breathing exercises.

My psyche was raw as I ventured into the mess tent, intent on curing my hangry mood. The warmers were full of chicken, veggie burgers, coleslaw, and salads. Filling up my plate, I thanked my lucky stars. It was a special day when they served coleslaw.

"Madeleine! Over here!"

Spotting Maisy and Trent at a table in the back, I joined them. There was one thing to be thankful for in Camelot—two *real* friends.

"We're glad you're back," Maisy said as I sat down. "I don't care what anyone else says."

I stared at her, my heart sinking despite knowing the truth of it.

"Maisy," Trent said with a groan, "I thought we agreed not to bring it up."

"Sorry." She shrugged and offered me an apologetic smile.

"Don't worry about it," I told them. "I'm well-aware of my standing around these parts. I'm so closely monitored, I doubt I'll be able to go to the toilet without someone watching."

Maisy wrinkled her freckled nose. "*Ew.*"

I widened my eyes. *"I know."*

"You seem…better." Trent tilted his head to the side and I felt his Light flutter.

"Stop it," I complained, the brush of Light making me shiver.

He straightened up, his cheeks flushing. "You felt that?"

"Yes, and don't ask me how. I hardly understand what I can do myself." And after that morning, I wasn't about to elaborate on the things I did.

Maisy suddenly looked interested. "Is that why you came back with Issac Worthington?"

I dropped my fork, thoroughly exasperated. "How have you heard of him and I haven't?"

"He's some hotshot spiritual scientist," Maisy said with a chuckle. "The things he can do with his Light…" She shivered, a giddy look on her face.

"Gross," Trent muttered.

"Why did we never see him at the Academy?" I wondered. "He had to be there while we were. He doesn't look that old. He would've only been a few years ahead of us."

"I heard he studied in New York," Trent said as he shovelled coleslaw into his mouth. "He did courses at one of those fancy human schools, too. Harvey or Howard or something."

"Harvard," I corrected. "He's English, though."

Trent shrugged. "Probably some exchange program."

Interesting. New York had been the hardest hit of all the Sanctums on the Dark Night. A picture of the arrogant, demon-hating, Issac Worthington was taking shape. If they stationed him in the U.S… *Forget it, Madeleine. Don't go digging.*

"I remember people making a fuss over it," Maisy said. "About Naturals not needing a human education."

"We don't," I stated.

"What kind of training are you doing exactly?"

"Issac thinks my abilities are linked to my emotions," I replied. "He wants me to *meditate*."

Maisy choked on her coleslaw.

"So, it's a glorified anger-management class?" Trent asked with a smirk.

I rolled my eyes. "Smart arse."

"Trent, do you have to?" Maisy complained.

"He's right, though," I told her. "Anger is a problem. At least that eye thing hasn't happened again."

"What eye thing?"

"The morning after the incursion, I got angry," I explained. "Wilder was sick and Ramona… Well, I got pissed off and my eyes went all dark. And there were these strange black veins spreading across my face." I traced beneath my eyes with my fingertips and shivered. "I don't want that happening again."

"A built-in early warning system, maybe?" Trent offered.

I shrugged. Knowing how these things usually went, I doubted it. "I don't know what to do," I admitted. "About Wilder, about me, how to handle it… It just seems too big for someone like me. You guys and me, it's only been a few years since we graduated. What do we know?"

"Some days I feel like I don't know shite," Maisy told us. "I think we all secretly fake it until we make it."

"Ditto," Trent told me. "Everyone's working on it, though. Aiden's got a whole team in the archive figuring out what might've made the Flames sick, and Thompson's got a whole squadron of Naturals to protect the city. Ramona's even got a permanent transfer now. The best of the best is here working on it, Mads."

"I didn't think things could get any worse," I murmured. "The hate, I mean."

"Let them worry about themselves," Maisy stated. "We have our orders and so do you. Who are we to argue with the Regula?"

"Exactly," Trent said. "You do you, Mads. We've got your back."

One day at a time…

"I have to report to Aiden at the archive after this," I said, picking at my lunch.

Maisy laughed. "You make it sound like torture."

"That's a pretty sweet gig," Trent countered. "I know a lot of people who'd love to see what's buried up there. Me included. Learning the forgotten secrets of our ancestors sounds like an adventure to me."

"Honestly, it's a double-edged sword," I added. "The vault is at the bottom."

"Anyone with half a brain can see it was the vault

and not you," Maisy said. "You were in the wrong place at the wrong time, is all."

"Yeah." Trent blew through his lips. "You, harm a Flame? That's the stupidest thing I've ever heard."

I laughed. "Thanks for the vote of confidence."

"That's the spirit!"

4

———

The archive was a hive of activity as I approached.

I didn't have a noticeable guard following my every movement, so I was a little reassured that I had a tiny piece of freedom.

They had blocked the edges of the rift off with ugly orange and white plastic barricades. In full daylight, the damage the cataclysm had wrought on the city was horrific to see. The castle was torn in two, the earth opening up into a maw of darkness so deep, no one could see the bottom. A portal had once opened up in its depths, but it was closed now. Instead of a gateway to another world, it was just a giant hole in the ground.

They had pushed the large metallic double doors which marked the entrance to the archive open all the way. It didn't escape me that this place might have been buried for a reason, the main one being whatever was in the vault at the bottom of the complex.

Curiosity had won out, though. We knew little of our history before the cataclysm, so opening this place was a temptation too important to ignore. The Regula seemed to agree and had ordered its excavation.

I passed through the doors and descended the stairs leading down into the first chamber.

Rows of shelving that reached to the ceiling were crammed into every available space. It was likely a foyer at some point, but the contents of the archive had spilled out here long ago.

Books and scrolls lay everywhere, covered in dust and cobwebs, though a small army of Naturals were busy cleaning and salvaging everything they could get their hands on. From here, doors opened into more rooms and passages.

Aiden was waiting for me at the bottom of the stairs.

"Hey," he said. "Good to see you back."

"You've been busy, I see."

"You have no idea. There's so much knowledge just in this room and it goes on and on into the hillside." He flapped his arms excitedly. "We're making a map of the complex, but it's slow going. We have to be careful of traps and other long forgotten security measures."

I glanced past him at the room beyond, half expecting poisoned spears to shoot up out of the floor.

"Don't worry," he added, "we've barely got past here and there are no booby traps...*yet*."

"Way to inspire confidence."

He laughed and gestured for me to follow him. "Let's walk."

We wandered through the foyer then down the hallway. I'd been here the night the Naturals had dug it up while in Ikakantor's thrall. Now it was lit up with rows of artificial lights, and it looked less spooky.

"We have to find out what the Dark wants," Aiden said as we descended to the next level.

"The vault," I told him.

"Yes, that's a possibility, but—"

"They want the vault."

He scratched his head and frowned.

"Whatever's in there made Wilder and Scarlett sick," I added. "They want what's inside the vault."

"That's all well and good," Aiden said, looking exasperated, "but we don't know what's inside."

I raised my eyebrows. "I'd advise against opening it."

"That's a bit of a paradox."

"I'll say."

"For now, we're focusing on trying to isolate the resonance," he went on. "That's why I asked for you. I mean, we need all the help we can get cataloging and mapping this place, but with things the way they are, the vault is taking precedence."

That's when I realised we were headed towards the bottom level.

"I can't go down there," I said. Freezing, my hand gripped the stone bannister and I stared down the flight of stairs into the unknown.

Aiden blinked as if he was in a daze. "Don't be ridiculous. Of course, you can."

"Aiden, you don't understand. My allies are few and far between. I can't do anything to make anyone doubt my intentions. If I go down there…" People would start talking and theorising on my behalf, no matter what.

"Madeline, I need your help." He placed a hand on my arm. "If we can seal up the vault and it helps Wilder and Scarlett recover, then everyone will see it had nothing to do with you."

I shook my head, hoping he was right. I needed a break, big time. "I was floundering before, but now I've been back less than a day and I'm already drowning."

"What would Elijah think?" Aiden asked. "He risked everything for you. You saved his life and he saved yours by bringing you back."

My gaze flew up. "How…?"

"I had a feeling," he said with a shrug. "You were so determined to find his cure, you risked everything."

I looked down the stairs. My hands were shaking. I'd been through worse than this, but now I had the power to prove everyone wrong. I was a work in progress, just like everyone else.

"Okay," I said. "Let's get to work."

Aiden gestured towards the stairs. "After you, then."

I descended into the murky light, trying not to rely on my power to guide me, using Aiden's Light ball instead. It was difficult to tune out all the negative voices and focus on the task at hand. It was too easy to fall into old ways, even with so much at stake.

We reached the landing in one piece, and ahead I saw some portable lights had been set up by the vault doors. Now that I could see them clearly, the gold and brass carvings and gears looked even more like a space-age clockwork puzzle. For something created in the Middle Ages, the locking mechanism was way beyond its time.

A man was waiting for us before the vault and it took me a second to realise it was my old Light Studies professor, Mr. Masters.

Hunched over a foldable table littered with books and papers, he looked exactly the same as I remembered him. Perhaps his hair was a little greyer, but the tall, surly teacher was a familiar sight amongst the unfamiliar surrounds of the archive.

It was a strange feeling, being seen as an equal to my teachers. After so many years under his thumb as an authority figure, it was difficult to wiggle out of the mould.

"Mr. Masters?"

He looked up and smiled. "Good to see you, Madeleine. I understand it's never a dull moment when you're around."

"Uh, I guess not."

"Masters is overseeing and developing the barrier to seal the vault," Aiden explained. "If anyone can crack this, it's him."

I looked up at the doors and wrapped my arms around my middle. My stomach churned and as I focused on the glint of metal in front of me, the more aware of the ebb of unknown power I became.

"You seem to be significantly more sensitive to Light and Darkness than we are," Masters said, noticing my uncomfortableness. "Once the barrier is in place, I hope you'll be able to sense if there are any leaks. Then we can tailor the design and placement as we go."

"We're thinking of layering the barrier," Aiden added. "The more Light we can weave around this thing, the more secure it'll be."

"Sounds like a plan," I said just to say something.

"Keep working with Issac and in no time, you'll be up to speed." I liked Aiden's optimism and went with it.

Footsteps echoed behind us and I turned. A woman around my age, with mousey blond hair, scurried towards us.

"Aiden?" The woman looked at me, not with dislike, but curiosity.

He turned at the sound of his name. "Yes?"

"Ramona wants to see Madeleine in the infirmary once you're done."

"Sure. Thanks, Amanda," he said.

I noticed her flush and she offered me a tense smile before hurrying up the stairs. A little spark of hope flared in my heart. Maybe things weren't as dire as I thought.

"I think I'll get you to assist Amanda tomorrow," Aiden said. "There's a learning curve, but you're smart. You'll pick it up in no time. In fact, it's not much different to digging."

I blinked and turned. "Huh?"

"Cataloging," he said. "Is the vault getting to you that much?"

"It makes me feel a little sick," I admitted. "Like I ate something bad or something."

"Interesting," Masters muttered, then scribbled something into his journal.

I glanced between them. "You don't feel it?"

"The air feels slightly charged," Masters replied, "but there's no nausea. I wonder why you can feel it and we can't."

"Do you think it has something to do with Wilder and Scarlett's sickness?"

Masters coughed, the sound causing Aiden to grimace. Their file was marked top secret, then.

"No one will tell me anything," I murmured. "Just that they're both in a coma."

I didn't even know where they were. Somehow, I knew it wasn't at the London Sanctum, but some place far more secret and secure. With a greater demon running around trying to break into Camelot —and likely trying to steal the very thing that took out the Flames—the Regula wasn't taking any chances.

"That's the basics," Aiden admitted. "We've been ordered to keep the details secret, otherwise…"

"I understand," I told him. "Need to know and all of that."

Aiden smiled and pointed to the door. "Now, can you tell us what else you feel?"

I wandered back to base camp, not in any hurry. After a long conversation with Aiden and Masters about the level of nausea the vault caused me, fresh air was filling my lungs. The archive was interesting and all, but it was stuffy and the air smelt like stale dirt.

When I entered the camp, I noticed a small lorry had arrived. It had backed up into the base camp and was dropping off a delivery of some kind. The back was rolled up and Naturals were unloading the contents, depositing boxes and other items onto the ground next to the infirmary.

I bypassed them and slipped into the tent. More equipment had been dragged inside, leaving the entire place in disarray. Looked like Ramona was getting some upgrades.

"Hello?" I called. "Is anyone alive in here?"

A flash of auburn hair peeked out from behind a crate and the doctor appeared. Ramona was always so put together, and it was amusing to see her so frazzled.

"Oh, Madeleine. There you are."

I stepped over some cases and slipped between two large black crates to get to her. "You wanted to see me?"

"Yes. I told them I wanted to see you first thing," she complained, "but everyone wants a piece of you."

"What's with the lorry outside?" I asked, deflecting the conversation onto other things.

"It seems we're at Camelot for the long haul,"

Ramona replied. "They're bringing in prefabricated buildings and equipment to build a temporary base."

I looked at the chaos around us and raised my eyebrows. "Wow, so it's a whole thing."

"It's the front lines now. Camelot is everything."

I staved off a shiver and sat on the stool beside the table. Before, the entire world had been a battleground. Demons had been doing whatever it took to search for a way to open the rift to let the rest of their kind through. Now it was all about the unknown in Camelot.

"Ikakantor is the first greater demon we've encountered in a long time," Ramona went on. "He's especially determined to get back into Camelot and that means all guns blazing for us."

"It's a wonder anyone's left at the Sanctum."

"I haven't seen this kind of response since the war." She clapped her hands together. "But we're prepared this time."

"Except Wilder and Scarlett—"

"Madeleine, stop frowning like that."

"Where are they?" I asked. "How are they? No one will tell me anything."

Ramona lowered her gaze. "That information is need to know… You know how the Regula works. The less people know, the safer they are."

I let out a frustrated sigh. "I just want to know if they're going to—" *Die*. It wasn't a word I wanted to say out loud, especially not where Wilder and Scarlett were concerned.

"As far as I know, there's been no change." She

gestured for me to sit. "There isn't much to say, anyway. No worse and no better."

I parked my rear on a stool. "Thanks."

She grinned and slid a tray across the stainless-steel table. It was full of medical equipment like individually wrapped syringes and needles, bandages, and antiseptic wipes.

I eyed a scalpel. "You're not going to do a live autopsy, are you?"

"No," she said with a laugh, "nothing that dramatic. I just want to do some basic blood tests. I'm hoping I can learn more about how the mutation has altered your genetic make-up. If I can understand it, maybe it can help you."

Shrugging, I rolled up my sleeve so she could stick me with the needle. I trusted her.

Ramona filled two vials full of blood—which came out red, thank the Light—and set one aside in a little refrigerator.

We watched the second sample spin in the centrifuge, the little vial blurring as the machine separated the different cells. Once the process was complete, the sample was removed and she used an eyedropper to make up slides to put underneath the microscope.

While they settled, she performed a full physical, shooing out Naturals who came in to drop off more boxes. She tested my reflexes, listened to my heart, read my blood pressure, and probed the edges of my Light. Finally, she scanned my soul, checking for any abnormalities.

Naturals and humans alike were susceptible to soul sickness—an illness directly related to possession or the overuse of Light. Demons who inhabited a body leeched energy from their host's spirit in order to survive, hence the sickness. Ramona, and doctors like her, were able to use their Light to heal and reverse the damage if it wasn't too severe.

My soul was unknown territory. I didn't know what she found, but if it was something serious, she didn't let on. All she did was record her findings like any other patient.

"Physically, you're healthier than you've ever been." She flipped through the results. "Your Light is still there, but so are the markers we identify in demons."

"You don't have to tell me that," I said. "I can feel it."

"You can? What is it like?"

"I tend not to focus on it."

Ramona smiled and nudged my arm. "C'mon. Tell me for science's sake."

I frowned, trying to think of the right words. "Well, it's like a constant push and pull. Maybe because I don't understand it yet. Mostly, it seems psychological, like the ultimate form of PMS."

"Like a war between identities," she offered.

"I'm neither, but I'm both."

"Interesting." Ramona pondered this for a moment, then added, "Then your work with Issac is even more important than we thought."

"He doesn't like me," I told her. "He argued

against me pretty viciously at the Regula hearing and now I have to spend all this time with him."

"Well, we can hardly blame him or anyone. The Dark consumed countless worlds before happening on ours, and the damage they've done here…" she trailed off with a shake of her head.

She didn't have to tell me. Everyone knew the death and destruction that followed creatures of the Dark. Knowing everyone thought my destiny was going to be just another chapter in that story was a kick in the guts.

"That's not who I am," I said softly, my heart hurting.

"I know it isn't, Madeleine."

"Power like this… It depends on intent," I argued. "There have been Naturals that have turned bad over the years. By their own choice, too. Things aren't as Light and Dark as some think they are."

"Have you tested your limits yet?"

"Give me a day," I replied. "I've barely had enough time to catch my breath."

"I'd say it's the same for everyone else. How can they understand what you are, when you don't, either? Right now, it's difficult to see through the what to the who. Give them time."

All at once, I felt exhausted despite the clear bill of health Ramona had just given me. "I wish things could go back to the way they were before I was mutated, but I can't go back…only forwards."

Ramona set down the tablet and busied herself clearing up the samples. "Where are you sleeping?"

I lowered my gaze. "Not in the barracks."

"I figured as much. You can stay here until you feel comfortable enough to go back."

"Thompson ordered me to—"

"I know what Thompson said," Ramona interrupted. "If he has a problem, he can come and argue with me. He's ten years younger than I am and the way he goes around—" She sighed sharply. "It annoys me to no end. Never get old, Madeleine. When the kids you remember teaching become your commanding officer, it really puts your mortality front and centre." Ramona was only forty, but she made it sound like she was ancient.

I gave her a half-hearted smile. That wasn't going to be a problem, not if Elijah was right about my state of the art, anti-aging soul.

"I just want to get through tomorrow," I told her. "Then I'll think about the next decade."

5

———

When I returned to the archive the next day, Aiden made good on his promise.

He introduced me to Amanda, who got down to work teaching me how to handle old books and scrolls without damaging them. We seemed to get along well enough, and she didn't shy away from speaking to me, so we got off to a good start.

Most of the books we were finding were old ledgers. Seemed to me that the topmost level of the archive was dedicated to official tax documents. *Boring.*

"Have you found anything interesting?" I asked.

"I swear it isn't as dull as all this. They had some really cool stuff," Amanda told me. "There are things here right out of a fantasy novel."

"Really?"

"For sure. They had these crystals that fit onto the sconces on the walls that Aiden thinks were full of

Light. They'd charge them up like batteries and they'd glow."

I glanced around the foyer and saw that she was right. There were sconces placed at regular intervals between the shelves and down the hallway, though they were empty now.

"I wonder why we stopped doing things like that?" It was such a simple solution that our dependence on modern technologies like electricity seemed silly.

"I supposed they stopped thinking about trivial things like that after the rift opened," she said with a shrug. "There were so few Naturals left and everything went into fighting the Dark."

"They should try quartz," I said without thinking. I remembered seeing rough chunks of it in the cave underneath Ben Nevis. Ikakantor had used it in his ritual to dig into my mind, but somehow telling Amanda that mightn't be the wisest thing to admit.

She lifted her head. "Quartz?"

"Clear quartz is meant to hold energy the best out of all crystals," I replied quickly. "I remember seeing it in a book back at the Academy. They're all supposed to have different energies for different things, but I just liked how they looked."

Amanda smiled, happy with my explanation. "They are pretty. My mother gave me an amethyst pendant once for my birthday."

I latched onto the small piece of personal information, hoping it meant she was warming up to me. "Really?"

"What about your parents?" Amanda asked. "Where are they?"

"My parents are on some secret mission. I don't know where they are."

"That sucks."

"Totally."

"So they don't know what's been happening with you and Camelot?"

"I don't think so." My thoughts went to them and I furrowed my brow.

If they knew about all the trouble I'd caused, and how my mutation was back, wouldn't they come and see me? They weren't even at the Regula hearing— not that I'd missed them. My parents had always been off on some mission or research trip since I was young, so our relationship was warm but indifferent. I'd learned from a young age to look after myself. It was the reality of being a Natural fighting a war that'd been going on for hundreds of years.

"Oh, I'm sorry," Amanda said.

"Don't worry about it," I told her. "I'm used to being isolated. I'm not exactly welcome anywhere these days. I'm half-Dark and everyone hates me for it."

She seemed surprised by my statement and blinked at me.

I flushed. "What?"

"I'm sure there are some people who think like that," she said, "but most don't."

"It doesn't feel that way."

"Mostly, they're intimidated by you," she added.

I paused. "Intimidated? By me?"

"You're powerful, talented, beautiful, and you aren't afraid to speak your mind. Who wouldn't be intimidated by that?" She brushed some dust off the table. "And you're friends with all the important people—Arondight, Jackson, Esme, Ramona, *Aiden*. You even stood up to the Inquisitor."

Amanda had a crush on Aiden, that was becoming clearer the more I heard her talk about him. The mere mention of his name had her flushing.

"I think it's because you're so apart from everyone else," she went on. "It's not your fault, I get that you feel pushed away by the things that happened to you, but it's like you think you're better than us."

"Better than you?" She may as well have just slapped me in the face. "I don't—"

"Warren was saying you used to always ditch your partner when you were at the London Sanctum."

"Who's Warren?"

She laughed and shook her head. "Exactly."

I isolated myself as a coping mechanism, not because I was arrogant about my abilities. Okay, so maybe I was up myself just a little, but now I understood why Wilder had sent me to Camelot. Not just for disobeying orders, but to bring me down a few pegs. Unfortunately for all concerned, I hadn't seemed to have learned that lesson until now.

The struggle for acceptance seemed futile, but it was clear I just had to try harder to reach out to the other Naturals.

"I was bullied the entire time I was at the

Academy," I confessed softly. "I guess it changed me more than I'd like to admit."

"It's tough for everyone," Amanda said. "That's life, but we can't let our bad experiences hold us back."

"So, no more breaking noses?" I asked with a grin.

"No more breaking noses," was her amused reply. "Though Rhys totally deserved it. He's such an arsehole."

I snorted. The high road wasn't going to be as sweet, but it did feel good giving him a taste of his own medicine.

"Thank you," I said.

Amanda blinked, taken aback. "Whatever for?"

"For telling me the truth."

Her surprise turned into a smile. "You're welcome."

A crash echoed through the foyer and we looked up to see Craig, one of the researchers from Australia, fall on his arse.

"Bloody hell!" he cried.

He was gathering a crowd and I went to see what he'd discovered. He'd been working on one of the doors leading off the main room. They were all locked, and of course, we were dying to know what was on the other side.

I stared through the open door into nothing and frowned as the surface began to ripple. Nothing was actually something.

"What in the world is that?" someone asked.

"It looks like water," another person declared.

The air seemed to disturb whatever was blocking the doorway and ripples fanned across the surface like waves on still water.

"It's a portal," I blurted. Everyone looked at me. "I've heard about them, but I've never seen one. That's what it has to be, right?"

"It sure looks like one," Craig said, agreeing with me. This seemed to put the others at ease and they began to chatter amongst themselves.

"Where does it go?" a woman wondered aloud beside me.

"It could go anywhere," Craig warned. "Be careful."

"Stand back," Aiden's voice boomed behind us. His approach scattered the Naturals and I looked at him with a new appreciation. Nerdy Aiden Thompson could be authoritative when he chose to be.

"I managed to decipher the locking mechanism," Craig explained as Aiden inspected the rippling wall of nothingness. "The door just flew open." He rubbed his arse cheeks and a few people sniggered at his misfortune.

"Has anyone touched it?"

"Nope," Craig replied. "Madeleine thinks it's a portal, and I reckon she's right. I don't know what else it could be."

"It is," Aiden murmured. "It's exactly like Scarlett described."

"Arondight?" Craig asked.

He nodded. "When she went to Avalon, she told me about the portals."

This seemed to excite everyone, and the chatter became louder, the sound echoing through the room. I doubted it was a portal to Avalon—the Lady of the Lake had sealed the realm forever once Scarlett had left. However, the thought was a little exciting, though.

"We have to secure the area," I said. "There's no telling where this goes."

Aiden nodded. "I agree. Craig, help me close this door."

The two men braced the large wooden door and heaved.

"It's a wonder you got it open," Aiden said. "This thing weighs a tonne."

I was watching on in amusement when a shriek pierced the air. We turned, my heart leaping into my throat as I saw Amanda's face contort in terror. She began to shake and her eyes rolled before her entire body became rigid. She was clutching a scroll in her hands, the parchment only partially unfurled.

I rushed towards her, intent to pry it from her hands, but Aiden shouted after me, "Don't touch her!"

Amanda shuddered and tears began to stream down her frozen cheeks.

"She's locked in a thrall," Craig said, standing beside me.

"It's the scroll," I said. "Can't you feel it?"

All eyes turned to me, but I was too busy feeling

out the power that radiated from the scroll clutched in her hands.

"Feel what?" Aiden asked. If he couldn't sense it, then it meant it was something Dark, or at least twisted beyond the bounds of Light.

"It's…leeching. Pulling…" I reached out for her and Aiden's panicked voice called out to me, but it was too late.

My hands curled around Amanda's head and my thumbs pressed over her temples. I blinked once and the room began to fade, and the second blink sucked me into the trance that was binding her.

Darkness swirled around me like a thick fog, clearing piece by piece as I adjusted myself to my surroundings. Images flashed past me like spectres, almost knocking me off my feet.

Spinning, I was dragged towards a twisting vortex. It reminded me of water rushing down a plughole, sucking everything down into the depths of whatever lay beneath.

Of course, I did the obviously stupid thing. I leapt into the torrent and allowed myself to be sucked under.

Amanda's mind was slippery, but I landed on both feet with all my spiritual limbs intact. Somehow, I knew I'd gone somewhere where no Natural had ever been before. There was connecting through Light and memory, but this was deeper.

Glancing around, I took in my surroundings. I stood on a large rock overlooking a wild and lonely moor. The air was full of ice, the chill seeping into my bones.

I was in a memory.

Wind tore at my hair as I took in the view, noticing large splotches of writhing black fog clinging to the rocky outcrops. They'd settled in the soggy ground, too. Whatever had taken Amanda had seeped into her deeper mind, creating a minefield of nothingness.

Was it trying to erase her? I shivered and wrapped my arms around myself. That's when I realised I wasn't Madeleine… I was Amanda.

I wasn't just in her memory, but I was living it first person point of view, just like I had with Issac.

Think, Madeleine. What did he teach me…

I didn't like the way his memory was unfolding, so I'd unconsciously changed the narrative. He was strong and had been aware of everything I'd been doing inside his head, but Amanda wasn't Issac. If I did that to her, there was no way of knowing if I'd change something permanently.

I had to peel myself away from her spirit and insert myself into her vision. Though that was easier said than done when I was winging it.

Conscious I was using the Dark part of my powers, I remembered Ramona's words of wisdom. *It depends on intent.*

I stepped backwards, away from the ledge, my spirit peeling away from Amanda's like Velcro. My 'skin' tingled, and I shook my body, attempting to rid myself of the strange feeling.

Amanda turned, her slender frame silhouetted by the sun. It had begun to set, lighting the sky with orange fire.

Her startled gaze met mine. "Madeleine?"

"Yes, I've come to help."

"Where are we?" She looked around, clearly confused. "How did we get here?"

"We're in the archive in Camelot," I said, wondering if this was a memory at all. She seemed aware she wasn't supposed to be here. "You touched a scroll and it brought you here."

"A scroll?"

"Yes. Do you remember what was written on it?"

She shook her head, the wind tearing at her mousy locks. "I don't remember any scroll."

Dammit. "It doesn't matter," I told her. "Do you know this place?"

"This was where…" She swallowed hard.

"Where what?" I prodded as gently as I could.

"My sister. She took…" Amanda looked towards the edge. "She jumped."

I sucked in a sharp breath.

The scroll must hold a curse or trap of some kind. The fog was erasing her memories and goading her subconscious into sacrificing itself. It was sick. The Dark had a lot to answer for, if it was the Dark's handiwork.

The fog was approaching across the moor, growing in size as it slithered ever closer. I glanced over the ledge and saw another heaving mass of black

Darkness below. It was consuming everything, eating away at her mind like acid.

Amanda edged towards the precipice and I held up my hands. "Stop," I said. "Think about this." If she jumped, she'd be lost. What that meant for me couldn't be good, either. "It wasn't your fault. It was her choice."

"I could have stopped her," she cried. "I ignored all the signs. I went away and she had no one with her."

"I doubt she would have wanted you to stop living your life."

"I abandoned her because I was sick of dealing with her problems. I wanted my own life and she took hers. *I'm a monster.*"

"You did everything you could, Amanda. It was her choice to take this path, not yours."

"I wasn't there," she sobbed. "I wasn't…"

I could feel her guilt simmering at the bottom of the cliff, urging her to jump.

"I'm with you now," I said, reaching out towards her. "Take my hand."

"*I can't.*"

I wiggled my fingers. "You can. We need you, Amanda. Aiden needs you. We'll never learn the secrets of Camelot without your help."

"He does?" she whispered, her voice was almost childlike as she stared at me with wide eyes.

"Yes, he does." It was a tiny fib, but I'd seen the respect he had for her. I didn't know if it would ever turn into something romantic, but there was a mutual respect there. To me, that was just as valuable.

Tentatively, she reached towards me just as the ground began to shudder. Her boots slipped and she began to fall towards the Darkness below with a panicked cry. I lunged, grasping her hand, and pulled.

We returned to reality with a gasp, and Amanda collapsed into my arms. The scroll fell from her hands and landed on the floor, rolling away into the murky darkness. She began to sob, holding onto me for dear life.

A commotion erupted around us as Aiden gestured to the other Naturals. Craig and another man extracted me from the inconsolable Amanda, attempting to soothe her hysterics.

"Get her to the infirmary as quick as you can," Aiden ordered. "We'll be right behind you."

They nodded and hurried from the archive, Amanda in Craig's arms.

"It was trying to erase her," I seethed, leaning over the table. I could feel the scroll somewhere behind me, pulsing on the floor.

"Erase?" Aiden asked, turning pale.

"Why was it just lying on a shelf?" I went on, my anger rising. "She could have been killed!"

"Madeleine." He placed a hand on my shoulder. "Careful."

I stilled at his touch and drew in a deep breath through my nose, using the breathing technique Issac had taught me. My lungs filled with the musty air of the archive, then I let it all out in one long whoosh.

"It was cursed or something," I explained. I told him everything I'd seen inside Amanda's mind, leaving out the part about her sister. Some things were private, and I knew I'd seen a part of her I probably shouldn't have.

"We've been arrogant," Aiden confessed. "Camelot was in the hands of the enemy for over eight hundred years. To assume their influence hadn't seeped into the archive was stupid." He clapped his hands, gathering everyone's attention. "I'm shutting the site down. Everyone out!" His bellow echoed around us as everyone stilled.

I was totally on the same page.

The research team began to gather their tools, leaving all the books and other artefacts where they lay. As they filed out, Aiden gestured for me to linger.

"If you weren't here, I don't think we could have saved her," he murmured. "I have never seen anything like that in my entire life."

I shrugged, unfamiliar with how to take his praise. "I did what I was trained to do."

"You can drop all the tough Natural warrior speak. You saved her life, Madeleine."

I nodded, my heart heavy. It could have so easily gone the other way, though.

"C'mon," he said, "let's get down to base camp. Ramona will want your help."

6

___

I stayed with Amanda through the night.

And it wasn't because that's where I was already sleeping, either. The young archaeologist had taught me a valuable lesson and I wasn't about to let her down when she needed me the most.

She woke a few times during the night, confused and disorientated. I was there to soothe her as Ramona worked to restore her memories.

She didn't remember, so I didn't remind her. What had happened with her sister was private and not for me to pass judgement on. If Amanda remembered and wanted to tell me about it, she would.

Ramona said the power binding the scroll had damaged Amanda's mind, but she was confident the fog would recede in time. Her amnesia would be temporary, thanks to my quick actions.

Aiden came to visit when dawn arrived. I left a wide-eyed and flushed Amanda in his care and went to meet Issac.

He was waiting for me outside his tent when I arrived.

"Let's go," he said, nodding towards Camelot.

"Where are we going?" I frowned, confused at his sudden change of tactics. I was ready for a day of singing Kumbaya—changing Lord to Light, of course—while sitting on pillows and holding hands.

"I've found somewhere outside where we can train privately," he replied.

I looked at the grey sky. "I think it's going to rain."

"Afraid I will beat you?"

I turned my gaze onto Issac. "We're fight training?"

"I knew that would get your attention."

I opened my mouth, but quickly shut it again. I wasn't complaining, not when it came with a private space hidden from hecklers.

Issac led me through base camp and into the lower city. I wondered what sacred space he'd found where Aiden wasn't going to give himself a hernia over us damaging priceless archeological relics.

"You're lively today," Issac said as we walked.

"I learnt a major life lesson yesterday," I replied. "It was affirming."

"The girl in the archive?"

"Amanda," I corrected. "And yes, she helped me learn something important and I was able to help her by using a new ability. You know, the one you're so afraid of."

"And what ability was that?"

I rolled my eyes. "Can we not pretend, Issac? You

know everything already. Your little birds are whispering in your ear twenty-four-seven."

"They also know you're sleeping in the infirmary."

"The other Naturals don't want me in the barracks," I told him, pushing up my sleeves. "It's better if I don't stay there. They need their rest if Ikakantor attempts to breach Camelot's walls."

"That's extremely considerate of you, Madeleine."

His note of sarcasm didn't escape me, but I ignored it.

"It's only been three days and already Camelot is a hive of danger and excitement," he added. "All the stories were true."

"You're welcome."

After a few twists and turns, we walked through an archway and stepped into a large, open space.

I looked around in surprise. It reminded me of a Roman amphitheatre with seats and a central stage, though it wasn't as round. In the centre was a narrow field of spongy grass and the tiered seating areas curved towards openings at either end. The open grass area looked about two hundred metres long and forty to fifty metres wide.

"It used to be a jousting field," Issac told me. "All the wood has rotted away but the stone is a foundation for bleachers."

"Jousting, huh? How Medieval."

"The area in the centre is called the lists." He handed me a wooden staff that he'd left in an alcove and took the other for himself. "There's room enough there for us."

"Are you sure about this?" I asked as I followed him down the stairs.

"Meditation can only get you so far, Madeleine," he replied, his voice echoing off the stone. "You must control yourself during times of high stress. That's when it's most important."

I began to stretch. "I already know that."

"In theory. Today is a practical experiment," he said. "I don't want you to use your abilities, just your physical strength and training experience."

I raised my eyebrows. "You want me to fight without Light?"

I wasn't even sure I knew how. Light to a Natural amid a life or death battle was everything. It was the edge that kept death at bay.

"The aim of this exercise is to control the use of your abilities," he explained. "Showing restraint is the first step towards breaking your reliance on what you can neither control nor understand."

I grunted, already annoyed. "I thought I was supposed to be testing my limits to see what I could do."

"Reaching your limit is dangerous when the power you have is out of your control."

Gritting my teeth, I gestured to his staff. "Have at it, then."

Issac assumed a defensive stance. "Remember, reign in your emotions."

We moved through a few drills together before we

switched to a free rein fight. His skill was impressive for a pencil pusher. He matched me on every strike and countered most of my blows.

"You're holding back," he said, catching his breath.

"I don't want to hurt you and get written up."

He snorted and we clashed again, this time with a little more ferocity.

"Elijah…" he said as we locked staffs. "What exactly is your relationship with him?"

"I don't know what you mean," I replied, my heart fluttering. I pushed against him, freeing my staff. "I told you everything at the hearing." Except the part where I suspected he'd once been a Druid and I had romantic feelings for him. I mean, Elijah was the first man to kiss me.

"Did you?" Issac gave me a look that said he saw right through me, but I wasn't falling for it. He didn't have a single shred of proof.

"I don't even know where he is. He could be on the other side of the world for all I know."

"Do you wish you went with him?"

"*Sometimes.*"

"Because you think he understands you?" Issac raised his eyebrows and leaned against his staff. "That's a dangerous admission."

I was tired of his baiting. Now his barbs were borderline threats and I didn't like it.

"Yeah, you know what?" I snapped. "He is the only person who understands me because he's the only other person like me."

"There's no one like you."

I narrowed my eyes and tightened my grip on my staff. "Then he's the next best thing."

I struck, forcing Issac to counter my blow. He wasn't ready and almost slipped onto his arse but recovered like a champ. For a spiritual science nerd, he knew how to fight like a warrior.

"You should train me to become a weapon for the Light," I stated as we locked together once more. "Without the Flames, the balance is in danger of tipping to the Dark. I could be the next best thing to Arondight and Excalibur."

Issac snorted and pushed back, breaking away. "Best not get ahead of ourselves."

"If Ikakantor attacks—"

"We know his name, Madeline. It's enough to bring him to his knees and imprison him. If he attempts to set foot in Camelot again, we're prepared to do whatever it takes."

"We've never captured a greater demon," I argued, "and it wasn't until Scarlett that we could kill one. I don't even know if a greater demon can be contained. Do you?"

"Let us worry about that," Issac said. "You need to worry about learning your abilities. We don't know what your full capabilities are yet."

Let's find out.

I attacked and Issac countered. Soon we were trading blows in a frenzied dance. I kicked this legs out from underneath him and he rolled to avoid the end of my staff. He flipped to his feet, then did a one-handed vault with the tip of his weapon to dodge a second strike.

Issac was fast, but he lacked the knowledge to counterattack. Honestly, I thought he spent too much time sitting on the floor with his eyes closed.

"Don't let your frustrations get to you," Issac said as we locked together. "Let them slide over you. You are more than your power."

I broke away and reset my stance, ducking when he didn't give me a chance to take a breath.

"Emotions get you killed," he went on.

"Lack of Light is what will get me killed," I fired back.

I felt my power simmer and wondered if I should just let it go. I was getting nowhere poking at the edges, hoping not to explode. Elijah said I didn't need an arondight blade to fight. Weapons were useless when my Light was enough. He'd wanted me to evolve and here I was, *evolving at a snail's pace.*

"Arrogance will get you killed," Issac snapped. *"Rein it in."*

Frustration had me gritting my teeth and I fought back, pushing him towards the edge of the arena. My unruly power filled my staff as I swung and slammed against Issac's with a clack, then splintered it clean in two. The force of the blow sent him flying and I dropped my weapon.

He landed on his back, the two pieces of his staff tumbling across the lists. I fell to my knees beside his stunned body and went to touch him but pulled back.

"I'm so sorry," I blurted. "I didn't mean…" He stared at the sky, silent. "Issac?"

"That was—"

"I didn't mean to." Despite helping Amanda, I knew my standing was still precarious in Camelot. If I angered Issac too much, he might report me to the Regula and all this would have been for nothing.

He sat up and rubbed the heel of his hand over his chest. "For once, I don't envy field work."

I was in a panic. "I said I was sorry. I don't know what else to do."

He lowered his head, catching his breath.

"The Dark has taken so many lives," he murmured. "The Dark Night tore families apart and almost drove us to extinction. I…" He shook his head. "We can't take any chances. You lost control and now we know."

His demeanour reaffirmed my suspicions that his hatred of me stemmed from something that had happened to him during the Dark Night in New York.

"I'm sorry for whatever happened to you, but I didn't do those things," I said.

His gaze snapped to mine, and his lip curled in anger. "While Darkness lives inside you, you'll never understand."

I rose to my feet, recoiling from his sharp words. "That's not fair. Do you really think I want to be like this? I don't. It was hard enough when everyone thought I was still a Natural. Shite, it was hard even before I was mutated."

"Your past is irrelevant, Madeleine. It is

meaningless." Issac pushed to his feet and brushed off his trousers. "Let's try again."

I bristled, the blow landing directly where he'd intended. He was crushing my spirit to control me, but it was going to backfire on him. I didn't know how, but it was the wrong tactic.

I felt the Darkness twist around my Light and I raised my hand to slap him, but he was faster. He wrapped his hand around my wrist and jerked me against his chest.

I blinked, then caught my breath. What the hell was I doing?

"This is going to take a lot longer than I first thought," he murmured.

"I assume that's a bad thing."

"Perhaps." His gaze lowered, brushing past my lips.

I shivered, the unfamiliar feeling of want flowing through my body. Me, attracted to the arrogant, hateful Issac Worthington? *Unlikely.*

"Your two sides are fighting for dominance," he said. "They must work in harmony."

"Like the Balance?"

He nodded. "It seems so, but it's up to you."

"What if I can't?"

He let go of my wrist and cupped my face in his hand. Running his thumb under my eye, I froze.

"You will," he said, leaning down to kiss me.

His touch was so unexpected, and I felt so frustrated and isolated, that I let him. Maybe a small part of me was attracted to his infuriatingly clean-cut brand of handsome and his position of power, but I'd never admit it. That or the fact that his kiss felt nice.

Something metallic clicked around my neck and I jerked away as a painful shock tore through my entire body. I gasped, the sensation almost bringing me to my knees.

I was cut off from my Light and the mysterious power I'd been trying to control.

I pulled at the metal collar with a wail, hardly aware of anything else around me. Losing something so fundamental to my existence was agonising and tears began fill my eyes.

"What have you done?"

"It's clear you can't control yourself," Issac told me, turning back into the harsh, judgemental, authority figure I loved to hate. "Measures have to be taken for the safety of everyone around you."

"You tricked me!" I cried. "I should never have trusted you!" He'd violated me in the worst possible way.

Something flickered through his eyes, but it was too fast for me to capture. "Until you can learn to harness your instabilities, the collar will remain in place."

I glared at him, hoping if I stared hard enough his head might explode. "You make it sound as if I have a mental disorder." I wiped at my mouth and spat on the ground. "I'll have you know that sexual harassment is a reportable offence."

He sighed and narrowed his eyes. "I apologise

profusely, but you would never have agreed to wearing it."

"You're damn right!" I tugged at the collar, but it was firmly locked in place. "No matter how many people I help, you will never see me any differently, will you?"

"There's so much you don't understand," he replied, cupping my face in his hand.

Ugh, men and their need to dominate the opposite sex was really getting on my nerves. Issac Worthington had manipulated me for the last time.

I struck like lightning, ramming my palm against the inside of his elbow. While his balance was compromised, I kicked his legs from underneath him.

Issac landed on his back, his startled gaze meeting mine. He couldn't blame it on my 'unstable' power this time. This was all me—pure, unpowered, Madeleine Greenbriar.

"No," I snarled, standing over him, "there's so much *you* don't understand."

7
———

I was so angry with Issac, sleep was impossible that night.

I tossed and turned, my legs tangling the blankets. The collar was uncomfortable and my neck ached something fierce.

A hand on my shoulder woke me some time in the early hours.

I opened my eyes and blinked, clearing the fog from my mind. A face stared down at me through the darkness and I hesitated.

"Elijah?"

He pressed his fingers to his lips to silence me. "Come with me."

"What are you doing here?" I hissed. "How did you get past the barrier?"

He shook his head and took my hand. Unable to stop myself, I padded barefoot across the infirmary and outside.

The base camp was wreathed in a thick layer of

fog. It crept between the tents, coiling around everything in its path, and muffling the sleepy nocturnal sounds of camp life.

Elijah was just as I remembered him—rough around the edges. His shaved head and stubbled jaw made him look handsome in a bad boy kind of way. Paired with his leather biker jacket, torn jeans, and combat boots made him a dangerous mix of demon and criminal.

"What's going on?" I whispered, wondering why my feet weren't cold.

"Wait and see, pretty spectre," he replied. Opening up the tent across from us, he dragged me inside.

The world went black, then erupted into a blaze of colour. We stood on the edge of a cliff, overlooking a lush green valley below. Trees carpeted the landscape and a stream sparkled as it snaked through the forest.

"Do you like it?" Elijah asked.

"Where are we?"

He stood beside me, looking over the valley. "A sacred place."

The air shimmered like a rainbow holograph and coloured light splintered across the vista. It was an oasis in a desert of war…but it was nothing more than a mirage.

"This isn't real, is it?"

"No," Elijah said with a shake of his head. "Honestly, I don't know what it's meant to look like."

This must be the world beyond the Darklands—

the Druidic homeland whispered in the myths and legends passed to the Naturals left behind on Earth.

"So I was right about you," I breathed.

"Truth is a fickle concept," Elijah replied, "but so is reality."

The longer I looked at him, the more I realised I was merely seeing what I wanted to see. "This is just a dream, isn't it?"

"You're speaking to your innermost desires," he whispered. "Not a bad ability to have."

"But Issac bound my powers. How——"

Elijah's expression darkened. "Who is Issac?"

"Are you jealous?" I spat. "You're the one who left me behind."

"That's so nice of you, Madeleine. Hate me for sacrificing myself to save your life. You still don't understand what you are. You're the most infuriating Natural I've ever met."

"If I knew I was arguing with my subconscious, I would've woken up hours ago!"

"The first step in getting the world to accept you is to love yourself first."

I threw my hands into the air. "Sounds like something I'd say!"

"But not listen to," he bit back. "How many times do I have to tell you, you don't need your silly toys."

I tugged at the collar around my neck. "This isn't a toy!"

"Wake up, Madeleine." He flicked me on the forehead and I blinked, startled by the childish movement. "Wilder saw what you were capable of and he locked you up because he understood that you didn't understand what he did."

"That's a mouthful…"

He gave me a look. "He took advantage of your ignorance."

"I knew I could get out of that prison," I exclaimed. "And *I did*. I'm not an idiot."

"You're the biggest imbecile I know."

I curled my lip. "Your demon is showing again."

"Wow." Elijah smirked. "Is it my demon…or yours?"

I hissed and looked away, turning my gaze back to the valley below. He was destined to travel to a place just like this with his people until the Dark took him. At least, that's what I believed. The real Elijah had yet to confide his truth to me.

"Madeleine, he will tell you when he's ready."

I looked up at him and shook my head. "Not until his demon side lets him back in."

"No regrets," he told me. "What you're facing is bigger than me. You're learning who you are so you can awaken the Flames. Don't forget what's at stake."

"I'd just like to thank myself for the reminder," I drawled.

"You're welcome." His lips curved up at one side in a way that made my knees weak. "You're a deep sleeper. I thought you would've woken yourself up by now."

"Me too…"

"Do you miss me that much?"

I nodded. "If this isn't real, then…" I lowered my gaze to his lips.

He raised an amused eyebrow. "You want to kiss yourself?"

"No. I want to kiss your memory. Is that such a bad thing?"

Elijah shrugged. "Only if you lose yourself in it and never wake up. You don't want to end up as a useless lump in a coma."

I scowled. "That's not fair. Scarlett and Wilder can't help it."

"You're the one who's thinking it."

"Dammit."

He laughed and pulled me into his embrace. "Forget about it. Everyone's secretly thinking it, though they'd never admit it to anyone's face."

He kissed me then, and it was the passionate touch I'd dreamed about ever since the night I'd kissed him on his deathbed.

I clung to him, wishing he was real, but he drew himself away, leaving my body on the edge of something explosive.

"That's enough of that," he murmured. "Do you really want your first time to be with yourself?"

"Then where are you?"

He smiled, already beginning to fade. "If you knew, you'd be the first to let yourself know."

I woke with a gasp, sitting bolt upright. The infirmary was in darkness, the soft glow of the medical equipment lighting the darkest spaces with a murky green hue.

Wiping at the sweat across my brow, I glanced at Amanda. She was still sound asleep, thank the Light.

Things were getting weird. Was I astral projecting myself into my subconscious now? I didn't even think it was a thing, let alone something I could do with the collar cutting off my abilities.

I sighed and lay back down. Staring at the ceiling, I couldn't shake the image of Elijah and the world beyond the Darklands. Whatever my mind was doing, it was unsettling.

If vivid dreams were the least of my troubles, then maybe Issac was right to collar me.

Maybe…

I glared at my reflection the next evening, studying the ugly metal collar in the mirror. The finish was smooth, though the edges were rough against my skin. I twisted it around, but there wasn't even a clasp or buckle I could even attempt to break.

Instead, I resorted to glaring again. My eyes had lost their brilliant blue hue after my soul had merged, so the steely grey irises made me look even more menacing than usual. Man, I could do tough really well.

"It's not going to fall off no matter how hard you scowl at it," Maisy said behind me.

Turning, I let my hand fall away with a sigh. The female bathroom was mostly empty, other than a cubicle at the end. Showering in a draughty tent wasn't the epitome of glamping, but at least the water was hot and the floor wasn't muddy.

"I did something good and I got rewarded with my powers being taken away," I grumbled.

"Aiden wasn't happy," Maisy said as she towelled her damp hair. She'd put on her black tactical uniform again, and her jacket hung on a hook behind her. "I heard him rip Issac a new arsehole."

"I know. Being able to sense stuff was one skill Aiden needed the most."

With Amanda still in the infirmary and me without my Darkness-sniffing power switched to on, I was pretty useless with cataloging a magical archive. I wasn't allowed to touch anything anymore and Aiden had given me a broom. *A broom.*

"I feel like a dog," I hissed, tugging at the collar. "And it rubs like hell."

She laughed. "Maybe I should get you a matching lead."

"It's not funny, Maisy. I can't even heat up my hands with my Light. I'm going to have to wear every item of clothing I own just to stay warm… and I don't own that much stuff."

"Now you know what it's like to be human."

"I hate him," I hissed. "I didn't even go to training this morning."

"Madeleine, you could get reported!"

"Oh, I'm just waiting for him to run off to the Regula and tell on me. He won't have a leg to stand on once I'm through with them." I pouted and went to tug at the collar again, but Maisy slapped my hand away.

"Stop that," she scolded. "You'll make it worse." She clucked here tongue and lifted the metal. "You *are* chafing."

I rolled my eyes. "Great. There goes my perfect skin."

"Here, let me see." She pushed my shoulders so I faced her. Her brow furrowed as she studied my face. "You look tired."

"Gee, thanks for noticing."

"Is something bothering you?"

I waited for the other woman to gather her things and leave the tent before

I scraped up the courage to speak.

"I couldn't sleep last night," I confided.

"You were dreaming?"

I nodded. "It felt like an echo, but I shouldn't be having any more of those." The echoes were an after-effect of Ikakantor's delving into my mind back when he had captured me. Somehow, I felt like I should be immune to those now that I was different. "Anyway, I don't think the collar will let any through."

"What was the dream about?"

I felt my cheeks redden.

Maisy's mouth dropped open as she assumed the worst, then she began to laugh. "Don't tell me you had a sex dream."

"No!" That only made my face flame brighter and I turned away.

"How did Issac get that collar on you anyway? You're too smart to let alone take away your Light. Wait… What do you call your powers? Is there a name for it?"

"I don't know," I replied. "Anyway, he kissed me, the pervert. A momentary lapse of judgement that will never happen again."

Her mouth dropped open again. "Issac *kissed you?*"

"Don't look so scandalised. It wasn't like that," I argued. "It was just a trick so he could put this stupid thing on." I wrenched at the collar, but it only dug into my flesh more. "I threatened to report him for sexual harassment."

"He doesn't seem like the guy who'd risk his career over a harassment complaint."

I shrugged. What did I know about men and romance? Nothing. I hadn't ever been kissed until recently.

"Madeline…" Maisy's tone was bordering on wanting to interrogate, so I admitted one of my greatest embarrassments before she wrung it out of me.

"I-I don't have any experience in those sorts of things." I lowered my gaze, thoroughly mortified. "No one wants to kiss someone who might be a demon."

"You've never been kissed?" Maisy seemed taken aback like it was the greatest scandal in the history of all Natural-kind. "Seriously?"

"*I've been kissed.*" I sank to the bench with a sigh. "Once." I was twenty-two, but right now, I felt like an awkward fourteen-year-old.

Maisy sat next to me. "Who was it?"

"Elijah."

Her cheeks paled. "Oh dear."

"He wasn't trying to manipulate me," I argued. "It wasn't like that. It was genuine."

Maisy shook her head and stared across the tent. "Man, this is so like a Romeo and Juliet thing."

"I think it's a little more complicated than that."

"And you had a sex dream about him last night."

"It wasn't a sex dream," I hissed, despite it being the closest thing to being one.

"But you dreamt about him?"

I sighed and slumped my shoulders.

"Do you miss him?"

I scoffed, "I don't even know where he is or if he's coming back." There were so many unknowns with Elijah, I didn't even know where to begin. Who was he, where was he from, how old was he, what were his intentions… The list went on.

"That's not what I asked." Maisy wasn't having any of my evasion.

I stared at my hands. "Yes."

"Hmm," she said thoughtfully. "Best not tell anyone you're in love with a demon-hybrid."

"I-I don't know about l-love," I stammered.

"I think you know more than you're letting on," she declared. "But I get it. They're not your secrets to tell."

"Why is this so hard?" I moaned. "Every day there's another scandal. And the kissing. *Ugh*."

"Welcome to the world of romance, Madeline," Maisy said with a laugh. "Just be thankful we don't have smartphones to wait by. At least Naturals *talk* to one another."

I offered her a flicker of a smile. I wasn't a Natural anymore, and Elijah was missing. He wasn't texting me, even on the demonic shortwave radio.

"Hey," Maisy said, rising to her feet, "do you want to go see if they have any leftover desserts in the mess tent?"

"Sure, why not?" A tub of ice cream sounded great right about now. "Just keep this to yourself, okay?"

Maisy nodded and pretended to zip her mouth closed. "My lips are sealed."

8

After a week wearing the collar, I still wasn't used to it.

Issac only took it off during training and blackmailed me into putting it back on once we were finished. The few hours I was able to get with my power wasn't nearly enough to soothe the loss I felt when they were taken away again.

The only good thing that happened was Amanda's memories returning. She was well enough to return to work in the archive—Aiden had reopened it, deeming the scroll thing an isolated incident—and I was alone in the infirmary again. I barely had enough time to catch up with Maisy and Trent, but they were just as slammed with work and training.

Camelot was quiet. For a city on the precipice of the unknown, it was strangely serene. Patrols came in and out, the wall was monitored, the Light boundary hummed softly, research went on in the archive, the dig continued in the upper city, and the construction of the prefabricated buildings were well underway.

And I walked amongst it, present but held apart from all the comings and goings. Elijah had called me a spectre and that's exactly how I felt.

Training with Issac had been a tense affair that morning, and I'd just spent my lunch break helping Ramona with packing up the medical equipment. Tents were being disassembled and personnel were already moving into their new buildings. At least it'd be warmer inside four solid walls than within the bounds of the khaki-coloured canvas.

I stepped out of the infirmary into the cool air of the Midlands. Temperatures in this part of the country plummeted this time of year and it wasn't uncommon for snow to fall as early as late September. With global warming becoming more of a thing, the notoriously bleak English weather was even more unpredictably damp.

I did a double take as I saw a familiar woman walking between the tents. Her raven hair was drawn back into a low ponytail and her pale skin and blue eyes were as brilliant as ever. She looked older than I remembered, but we all were.

"Mum?"

Her gaze met mine and she came to meet me.

"Madeleine." She drew me in for a hug and I stood like a plank of wood and took it.

I stared over her shoulder, my voice soft. "You're not afraid of me?"

"You're my daughter," she said, pulling back. "Of course, I'm not."

My lips thinned. That's what parents were supposed to say.

"Your eyes…they're grey."

"A side effect." I shook my head. "What are you doing here?"

"Greer is visiting Camelot," she told me. "I have a report I need to deliver to her, and she requested we meet here." She smiled and took my hand in hers. "I think she had an ulterior motive, though."

Her answer was conflicting. Had she wanted to see me, or was it just a matter of circumstance?

"It's been two years," I muttered. "You haven't written or called once."

"Your father and I…" She sighed. "Our work is highly confidential."

I raised an eyebrow. "And you show up now?"

"This was the first opportunity I had. When we heard about your…" I noted she couldn't say the word mutation. "We did everything we could to come to Camelot."

It was my turn to sigh. There was no point in arguing over it. Family was important to the Naturals, but all bets were off when it came to maintaining the balance. While Darkness remained, their work would always take precedence.

"After everything you've been through, to have this happen…" Mum trailed off and offered me a sad smile.

"It's not so bad," I remarked. "Nothing has changed really. I'm still treated the same."

She raised her hand and ran her fingers over the collar around my neck.

"Don't," I said, moving away. "It's humiliating."

"It's necessary. What if you lost control and hurt someone?"

I lowered my gaze, feeling as if I was five years old again. "How can I lose control of who I am?"

"Lots of Naturals have lost themselves. We are still human at our core."

"So my babysitter keeps telling me."

"Are you making any progress?"

I shrugged. "I guess. I can still use my Light."

"And this…demon man. Has he contacted you?"

"*Mum*," I exclaimed. "Now is not the time to parent me about boyfriends. You should have done that when I was fifteen."

"Who said anything about boyfriends?" She raised an eyebrow and I suddenly got a glimpse of my future self, which only rubbed in my condition. I didn't know if I was going to grow old enough to have a wrinkle. Not even Issac had come to the conclusion Elijah had.

"At least he wanted to know me," I muttered. "He trusted me. That's still in short supply around here."

"Madeleine, demons lie. It's their nature."

"Not you, too." I shook my head.

"You need to be careful where this boy is concerned. The Dark wants Camelot and they'll do anything to get it back."

"You don't understand. No one does." I buried

my hands into the pockets of my jacket. "Maybe Scarlett and Wilder would, but they're both in a coma. Elijah was the only one who didn't look at me like I was a danger to myself and everyone around me. He challenged me to grow and see my potential."

Mum pursed her lips, clearly wanting to say something. Whatever it was, I didn't want to hear it. I had enough voices biting at me already.

"What do you know about the vault?"

"Nothing," I replied. "You best talk to Aiden and Masters about that."

Movement in my peripheral vision startled me and I spun. Cursing at the sight of Issac, I glared at him. "Don't do that. You know I can't sense you with your torture device on."

He smirked at me, then turned to my mother and gave her the warmest smile I'd ever seen on his posh, uptight face. I blinked, wondering if I was looking at the same guy. He was wearing his posh coat, but underneath he wore a standard tactical uniform with muddy combat boots.

"Issac," Mum exclaimed with a wide smile, "it's good to see you again."

He nodded once and glanced at me. "Mrs. Greenbriar."

Mum waved him off with a chuckle. "How many times do I have to tell you to call me Bethany?"

I narrowed my eyes and looked between them. The familiarity they were showing one another was highly suspect, not to mention annoying.

"What brings you to Camelot?" he asked.

"Greer," she replied. "It's report time."

"Any progress?"

"Some."

I stood there like a lump, pushed out of yet another conversation about top secret bureaucracy. At times like these, I wished I still had my arondight blade, a cold iron dagger, an area of London to patrol, and a partner to ditch.

"Some is better than none," Issac said. "Are you going up to the archive?"

"Yes. I'd like to see what's happening with that bothersome vault. I hear they're no closer to finding out what's creating that energy."

"Unfortunately, it's a real puzzle."

I sighed and crossed my arms over my chest.

"Do you want to come with me, Madeleine?" Mum asked as if she'd just noticed me.

"I've got duties to attend to," I lied.

"Of course. I'll see you at dinner?" I nodded as she kissed me on the cheek. "It's good to see you, you know."

"Sure thing."

She pursed her lips and nodded at Issac before she made her way through base camp.

Issac didn't move, much to my annoyance. He just looked at me all judgemental like, but that wasn't anything new.

"So, the loathing doesn't extend to my mother, I see," I drawled.

He grunted and didn't grace me with an answer.

"She obviously thinks the sun shines out your rear

end," I went on. "Why haven't I met you before now, I wonder?"

"I have a working relationship with your parents," he replied, "nothing more. It's not like I'm invited around for tea."

He was cagey, which meant he knew something I wasn't supposed to. Or there was a personal stake in the relationship.

"Then you know what work they're doing," I commented, aware he wasn't going to tell me anything. Issac liked to follow protocol down to the finest detail. And he was highly strung.

"You can ask all the questions you like, Madeleine, but I can't give you any answers."

"There's a lot of that going around lately."

I wished I was closer with my parents, but there was a demonic mutation and a secret mission in the way.

I sighed. "You're so uptight. It's a wonder your head hasn't exploded from all the self-imposed stress."

"My work is important and so is yours," he replied. "We all have our parts to play, no matter what secrets we need to keep."

"I can always trust you to answer with philosophy."

His lips quirked ever so slightly before he changed the subject. "Is Aiden expecting you this afternoon?"

I gave him a filthy look. "Until I'm allowed to use my abilities, Aiden has me cleaning mud off broken pottery. What do you think?"

He grunted and delivered a line I'd never hear

him say in my entire life. "You can go to the archive or we can have another training session."

"Wait… You're giving me a choice?" Skeptical was my middle name today.

"You've been improving," he replied. "I'd like to build on that, but if you want to spend time with your mother…"

I looked after her and shivered as the wind stirred. Melancholy tugged at my heart as I released we'd grown apart. Who I was becoming was excising me from everything and everyone I cared about.

Alone in a crowd.

"I'd rather have some time to myself," I said to Issac. "I need to think."

"That's not exactly within the bounds of your probation."

"Probation? Is that what we're calling it now?"

"*Madeleine.*"

I tugged at the collar. "What can I do without my powers? Nothing. I'm as feeble as a human."

"With military-level fight training."

I smirked and wiggled my eyebrows. "Watch out, then."

Issac deliberated silently for a moment, his brow furrowing. "Go on. Don't forget to sign in at dinner, though."

"Gee thanks, Dad." I rolled my eyes and made my getaway before he changed his mind.

"Hardly," he muttered as I walked away.

I ventured into Camelot, leaving base camp behind.

The lower city was a warren of alleys and crumbled buildings. Some parts had been excavated, but most areas were as wild as the day the demons had left. Nothing lingered here anymore, though it was still unknown territory.

Needless to say, I went where no Natural had been in hundreds of years.

I ducked through an arched doorway and found myself in what used to be someone's house. A fireplace was set in one wall with soot still blackening the stonework. Any wood that had been built into the structure had long since rotted away making the sky visible overhead through the first and second story. Lonely windows sat high up and I was left wondering what it might have been like to live here.

I ran my fingers across the moss growing between the stone blocks and thought the tiny fern which clung to a grain of dirt looked rather cute.

The silence here was deafening. I listened to the wind rush through the empty buildings and shivered. Good thing I didn't believe in ghosts, but after all the things I'd seen in this world, I wouldn't be surprised if they were real, too.

Running my hand along the wall, I paused when I saw some marks carved into a small stone in the wall beside the fireplace. It appeared to be a rune, Druidic perhaps. It was merely a simple 'x', but I knew from Aiden's history classes that they meant more than just 'x marks the spot'. However, here it seemed to have the latter meaning. The stone was loose.

I pried it out of the wall, revealing a hidden hidey hole. As I reached inside, my Light sparked and I snatched my hand back with a yelp.

Man, that stung.

Curiosity got the better of me and I reached into the hole once more, this time trying to avoid getting shocked. My fingers brushed against something hidden within and I pulled it out.

A pendant sat in my palm, the beaten and polished metal cool to the touch. It was a shield with three gold crowns of a field of silver—the Pendragon coat of arms, and the symbol of the rulers of Camelot.

Someone must have hidden it here for safekeeping. Whoever they were, I silently thanked them and the Light that they'd used to protect it from sticky fingers like mine.

I reached inside myself, dragging the spark I'd felt earlier to the surface. Light pulsed within me and I gasped as my abilities rushed to the surface, fully operational.

Issac's fancy power-blocking collar was useless. I began to laugh at the simple stupidity of it all, the sound echoing through the abandoned streets.

All the time Elijah had been pushing me to evolve, I never realised it was my own mind getting it the way of realising my full potential. I never needed the collar. It would never block anything but because I believed it, it was true—just like those times Trent had seen through my invisibility.

I wondered if Issac knew. Spiritual Light was his

speciality, but it didn't seem to matter as long as I didn't reveal myself as a threat. If trust was what he wanted, then trust was what he'd get.

Madeleine Greenbriar, actress. It had a nice ring to it.

Despite my newfound awareness, I let some power trickle through my veins, warming the chill in my bones, and climbed up onto the wall. From my perch on the side of the crumbled building, I could see across the outer wall of Camelot to the countryside beyond.

Thankful for the moment of silence, I watched the sun set over the Clee Hills as long as the golden rays radiated through the stormy clouds. Below, I counted the lights of the human city sparkling through the veil and wondered what would happen next.

Whatever it was, it wasn't going to be good. That was the only thing I was certain of.

9

———

Base camp was a hive of activity the next morning. The convoy carrying the acting Inquisitor was due to arrive within the half-hour and everyone was busy making final preparations.

I didn't know how they could polish the turd that was a muddy and haphazard building site into something resembling a Renaissance painting, but a small army of Naturals were giving it their best shot.

I stood on top of the wall, leaning against the parapets. The valley around Camelot was half in shadow as the sun rose—the early morning light wouldn't fill all the dips and dales until midday—and I focused my gaze on the rough track which led from the main human roads. At least someone had been out with a lorry full of gravel filling potholes—the modern-day equivalent of throwing a jacket over a puddle.

I felt Issac approach behind me and to my surprise, I was indifferent about it. Did that mean I was warming up to the guy? I wasn't sure, though I was getting used to him being around.

The wind rose, whipping colour into my pale cheeks. At least I was warm, and Issac still hadn't figured out his demeaning collar was useless. It wasn't like I was going to use it against him. Well...maybe just a little.

He stood beside me and followed my gaze. He was wearing his fancy Burberry knock-off coat and his hair was buffeting back and forth, his usual artful style all messy. "Nothing yet?"

"No." I checked my watch, but forgot I wasn't wearing one. It'd stopped working around the time I began changing. The irony wasn't lost on me.

"How was dinner with your mother?"

"Awkward and dull," I replied with a huff. "She can't tell me where she's stationed or what she's doing. Work is her life, so it leaves little to talk about. Same goes for my father."

"You have a lot going on," he offered.

"She wants to talk about that even less." I looked out across the valley, but there was no sign of the convoy yet. "Imagine being a celebrated Natural and having a half-demon screw-up for a daughter."

"I don't think it's that dire."

I shot him a skeptical look. "What? You're being nice to me now?"

"Family is important."

I grunted. "She likes you. Maybe they can rush through the adoption papers."

"Are you really that distant from one another?"

"You're the son they wished they had," I told him. "Put together, successful, never gets into trouble, earns great money, can look after them in retirement… I'm none of those things."

"You've achieved great things, Madeleine. Things any parent would be proud of."

I scoffed, "My parents are indifferent to me."

"Your mother loves you," Issac countered. "I saw it yesterday."

"She loves me in her own disjointed way. But do they love me enough to help me through this? I'm changing into something not even I understand and all she wanted to talk about last night was that heap of rubble." I jabbed a finger at the castle behind us. "Then there were the long stretches of awkward silence. No…" I shook my head and leaned against the parapet, "I'm alone with this and that's just how it is."

Issac moved closer. "You're not alone, Madeleine."

"Next thing you're going to say is that I've got you." For as long as I'd live, I'd never forget the awful things he'd said to me at the Regula hearing.

"Yes."

I looked at him and raised my eyebrows, not sure I wanted to hear what he had to say next.

"I was wrong about a lot of things," he murmured, the wind tugging his words away.

I had a prime opportunity to rub it in, but I held my tongue.

"I see how you're treated and I know it can't be

easy," he went on. "You've shown great restraint since we've been working together."

Issac was praising me? I didn't know how to take a compliment, so I just looked away.

"You never told me how old you are," I stated, glancing back at him.

He smiled and leaned against the parapet. "Old enough to know better."

"That's not an answer."

"Sure it is."

"An evasive one, maybe."

He laughed, looking annoyingly handsome. "I'm twenty-seven."

I looked him over. "Interesting."

"What's that supposed to mean?"

I smirked and turned my attention back to the valley. In the distance, I caught the glint of sunlight hitting metal. "The convoy is coming."

Three black sedans approached along the track, moving at a glacial pace. The road wasn't designed for the delicate suspension of a town car, so it was like watching a snail cross a busy footpath—irritatingly slow.

Coldness seeped into my bones and I looked towards the horizon, my entire body rigid. Something was coming…

"What is it?" Issac asked with a frown.

"Demons," I said a split-second before a swarm of black figures appeared on the ridge above Camelot.

Issac straightened beside me and the base camp alarm system began to wail. The barrier flared, sending a wave of golden Light shimmering before us, rippling outwards as it encased the outer perimeter of the city.

"The convoy," I breathed, my heart hammering in my chest. My gaze flickered between the three cars on the track, across the open expanse of the hillside, to the sharp ridge where the demons stood. They were moments away from careening down the slope and overwhelming the Naturals below.

Men and women piled out of the cars, forming a protective ring around the central car—the one holding Greer. They knew they'd never make it to the city in time, but it was ten against fifty… *at least*.

Without Greer or the Codex, the Naturals would be lost.

"Take off the collar," I demanded, grabbing Issac's arm. He didn't need to, but I selfishly wanted to preserve the little spark of trust he'd begun to foster for me.

He hesitated.

I shook him. "They'll be overrun before backup can get to them. We're closer." The demons began to spill over the ridge, revealing their numbers were far greater than I'd estimated. "*Issac.*"

Reaching up, he removed the collar and tossed it to the ground. "Go," he said. "Be safe."

I nodded, his words not registering beyond 'go', and vaulted over the parapet.

I landed, my boots digging into the soft ground eighty feet below the top of the wall, and pushed off at a sprint. I didn't care that I didn't have an arondight blade or a weapon of any kind. My only thought was heading off the horde.

I skidded to a halt, realising I'd crossed the distance in mere moments. How or why was beyond me and I turned.

I stood on the open field, a lone figure against a screaming army of horror. Behind me, I was vaguely aware that the Naturals protecting the convoy were yelling at me, but they didn't understand.

Now that I was facing the greatest battle of my life, I finally understood. *I understood what I held inside me.*

Everything faded and the world slowed. I took a step forwards, the galloping demons racing ever closer. The ground shook under my feet and I straightened my fingers, stretching out my hands to the earth.

One against a hundred.

The wind tore at my hair as I stared into the face of death, nothing standing between me and the razor-sharp claws of the distorted humanoid demons. Their shrill cries echoed across the hillside as they called to one another in a strange animalistic language.

I grabbed hold of the unknown and dragged it towards the surface. Heat began to build in my palms and my breath came in short, ragged gasps.

All that mattered was killing demons.

The earth erupted, splintering towards the enemy. They broke stride, almost falling, but carried on as the ground began to glow red and orange—the colours of Hell itself.

Then…the hillside ruptured, spewing forth a torrent of magma that spit into the air.

I'd called on the fire of the Earth and it had answered.

Demons fell into pits of lava, screaming and wailing as they were dragged under. They burst into flames and ash swirled into the air, carried away by the wind.

I swept my arm to the right, opening the chasm across the breath of the advancing vanguard, then to the left. Their way was blocked but the demons never broke stride.

With a cry, I let go of everything that tethered me to Madeleine Greenbriar and her petty insecurities, and raised my arms, unleashing the depths of my soul with a ravaged shriek.

The Dark would not take Camelot. *Not on my watch.*

As the demons attempted to leap the chasm, a wall of solid lava shot into the air, consuming the horde. Their screams were severed as the Earth swallowed and purified their poison, and as I lowered my arms, so did the curtain of fire.

Lava settled back into the chasm, splashing and bubbling as it devoured the last of the army.

I gasped, catching my breath as ash began to fall from the sky like snow. The rich green hillside had become a smoking pit of fire and death.

What have I done?

Shrieks pierced the air behind me and I spun, gasping in horror as one of the Naturals was torn in two, his parts falling to join the remains of the other nine guards. A hulking man stood before the central car, his body covered in blood and gore. It was a Colossus, an eight-foot-tall chimera of flesh, bone, and brute force.

This one wasn't as mindless as the one who had attacked the Academy all those years ago. It had a host, and I knew who inhabited the monster before his gaze met mine.

Ikakantor.

Rage exploded inside my body and I ran towards him, forgetting about the destruction I'd already left in my wake. *This was what Wilder was so worried about.* If I lost control, Camelot would cease to exist.

Right now, I didn't give two flying f—

I picked up a hilt from one of the fallen Naturals and it erupted into life, the links clicking together in a shower of silver and red sparks. Swinging, I pirouetted around the Balan, the blade slicing and hacking as I circled the creature.

Ikakantor fell to his knees, dazed by the flurry of attacks, his heavy limbs too slow to keep up with me. He didn't feel any pain, but it didn't matter. If all his tendons were severed, he could never walk out of here.

Landing on the roof of the car, I pointed the blade at him. "You will not touch her."

"Do you like my new body?" he asked, smirking up at me. The top of his head reached my waist, but the flesh of his meat suit was still soft enough to cut off his shoulders.

"It's *disgusting*."

"I see you've learned how to use the gifts we gave you," he rasped.

"*Ikakantor*." My power simmered as his name rolled off my tongue.

The Balan shuddered, his glamours flickering to reveal the grotesque state of his sewn-together body.

"*Wow*," I drawled, "you actually tried to glamour some of the ugly out of your latest meat suit to impress me? You shouldn't have!"

He cried out, his voice echoing across the hillside. "You *dare* use my name against me?"

"Oh, I dare." I tightened my grip on the hilt of the sword. "And I know what I'm capable of now. You can't have the vault. You can't have Greer. And you can't have me. Camelot belongs to the Light and so does this world."

"You belong to me!" The car shuddered with the force of his anger, but I held steady.

I had to hold on to my anger, otherwise I'd risk hurting Greer. Everything Wilder and Issac had tried to teach me clicked into place like it never had before. And to think, all it took was turning a valley into a volcanic caldera. One day I wouldn't be so slow on the uptake.

I curled my lip at the Balan. "That's no way to win a lady, *demon*."

Ikakantor laughed, blood oozing from his joints. "Come down from there and we can talk. I have something important to tell you, Madeleine."

"They only way this is ending is with your true death, Ikakantor."

He grimaced as his name rippled through him. "If that's how you want to play it, then fall to your knees, *Eilhana.*"

My entire body jolted, and I gasped as the air whooshed out of my lungs. I fell as all the strength left my body and tumbled off the roof to the ground. I landed face-first on the gravel, my power slippery to the touch. Gasping, I couldn't grab hold of it.

"Madeleine!" Greer shouted, reaching for the door.

"Stay inside!" I cried, holding out my hand.

Ikakantor knelt over me, his bulk casting an impossible shadow. "It doesn't feel so good, does it?"

"Eat shite, you ugly son of a—"

"*Eilhana,* you know better."

Pain stabbed through my mind, taking my breath away. Eilhana? He'd threatened me with the existence of a true name once before, but I'd laughed in his face. Demons loved to lie, but as it turned out, he was actually telling the truth.

Dammit.

"Do you want to know about the greater demon from who you originated?" Ikakantor asked. "I knew her well until your Indigo Flame murdered her."

"Scarlett…" I clawed at the ground, unable to gather my wits.

"Eilhana was a great heroine of the Dark," he went on, smirking as the name twisted my insides. "She developed the first iteration of Human Convergence. If she could see you, Madeleine, she'd be so proud. We could never fight the Flames of the Light, but with you…" He laughed and stroked my hair. "Oh, with you we could rule this world. We never needed the One to lead us. Not when we could create our own power."

"I'd never help you," I rasped. "I'd rather die."

His expression darkened and he glanced up at the car where Greer was trapped, helpless. "Not yet. First, I have to reintroduce you to your true calling, Eilhana."

I grabbed at any power I could hold on to, gathering it close. My senses began to return and I felt Light approach from Camelot.

"My. Name. Is. *Madeleine*." I lunged, grasping his fleshy arm, and pushed all the power I could gather into him. He cried out, then sparks tore through his neck.

Ikakantor's head flew off his shoulders and bounced onto the gravel track, rolling to a stop in a pothole.

Black smoke poured out of the useless body, gathering in the sky overhead. The cloud crackled with angry red electricity, but there was nothing I could do to stop it from gathering. Ikakantor lived on like a cockroach after nuclear Armageddon had decimated the world.

I covered my face, curling into a ball as what was left of the Balan's latest mortal incarnation burst into a ball of flame. Heat radiated against my forearms, but it was gone just as quickly.

"Madeleine," Issac knelt over me, his arondight blade clicking back into its hilt, "are you all right?"

I nodded as my powers began to return and let him help me to my feet. The bodies of the fallen Regula guards littered the surrounding ground, blood seeping into whatever was left of the lush green grass. The hillside was a smoking ruin, the lava I'd called already cooling.

Greer climbed out of the car and took up an arondight blade from one of her fallen guards, her face a mask. "His essence is gathering more demons."

We circled the decimated convoy and looked towards the horizon. Again, I sensed what Greer had before the enemy crested the rise.

This time, there were more Dark creatures and I wasn't sure I had enough power left for a repeat performance. The understanding I'd felt earlier had faded and dread now sat in place of the serene calmness of absolute power.

Reinforcements from Camelot lined up behind us, their arondight blades shining with silver fire. The cavalry had arrived… and not a moment too soon.

10

———

We faced off against the horde of demons as they stood on the ridge, screeching their twisted battle cries. Ikakantor's essence heaved above them, gathering their strength.

Issac pressed his cold iron dagger into my hand.

"I don't——" I began, but he shook his head.

"I know, but you have to arm yourself with something."

"Do you think you're strong enough for a repeat performance?" Greer asked me.

I shook my head. "I'm not sure I have the strength or the understanding. With this many Naturals on the field, I don't think I should risk it."

Greer nodded, then turned to the warriors. "We must protect Camelot," she shouted. "*At all costs.*"

"For the Light!" someone screamed, creating a wave of echoes from the others.

"For Camelot!"

The demons screeched and wailed as they trampled down the slope. They were in a frenzy, their barbed tongues lolling as they tasted blood in the air.

Fifty Naturals against two hundred super demons with razor-sharp claws seemed like insurmountable odds, but we'd faced worse. Besides, I had some new tricks of my own.

The assembled arondight blades cast an eerie silver glow over the ashen hillside as the Light let out their battle cry and sprinted across the field to meet the enemy.

The two sides clashed, cold iron slicing through Darkness and claws ripping apart flesh. Screams mixed with cries of anger and I dove into the fray with single-minded purpose.

Ikakantor's essence flared above us, guiding and empowering the demons as they fought. When the field split from the two battle lines, things became blurry. Demons and Naturals scattered across the open space—fireballs exploded and ash fell, the glare of Light infused swords blinding in the chaos.

I ducked and swung, pirouetted and leapt, cutting down demon after demon. The dagger stabbed into flesh and my power ripped apart what was left. There was no time to take a breath…to do so was death.

A scream tore at my concentration and I spun just in time to see a sharpened claw take a Natural's head clean off. I staggered, the sight tearing at my insides, and I was knocked flat by a frenzied demon, Issac's dagger flying out of my hand. A foot slammed into my back and I cried out, my power flowing into me with reckless fury.

I pushed off the ground, unnatural energy launching my body high into the air, and I landed on the creature's back. As it tried to dislodge me, I sent a pulse of power into its head. It exploded into a fireball, the flames singeing my clothes as I landed on my feet in a cloud of ash.

I snatched up a fallen Natural's arondight blade and the links clicked together in a shower of silver and red sparks. Movement at my left sent me pirouetting out of the reach of another set of claws and my blade flashed as it severed an inky black arm. Then I twisted, bringing the blade around in a wide arc and hacked its head from its slimy shoulders.

Heat exploded behind me and I was clear for a blessed moment. I couldn't see a damn thing through the ash and smoke. Wherever Greer, Issac, and the others were, I hoped they were okay.

Looking towards the sky, I spotted Ikakantor's essence swooping at the battle below, buffeting Naturals. He passed through a warrior who dropped his blade and began to convulse as a demon on the ground galloped towards him.

He fell to his knees, and I realised it was Rhys. The man who'd tried to lead a Lynch mob against me. The man who hated me for being part demon. A man fulled by prejudice. He was a bully and a bigot, but I couldn't leave him.

I cried out and rushed towards Rhys as he fell. I hurdled over his shuddering body and collided with the demon, the force sending us rolling down the slope. I lost my sword again as my body hurtled through the air, pummelled by rocks and the massive bulk of the demon.

I landed with a thud, the demon rolling a few more times before it recovered and turned towards me. Ignoring the pain that throbbed through the hundreds of cuts and scrapes on my exposed skin, I rose to my feet.

Elijah was right—I didn't need a sword to kill demons anymore.

A second demon joined the first and I curled my lip. A third and fourth loomed out of the smoke and ash, then a fifth and sixth formed a cage. They circled me, barbed tongues licking and tasting the air.

"It is her," one croaked.

"He wants her," another said.

"We will take her."

"Like hell you will," I snarled.

"Hell," the first demon cackled. "You will know Hell, creature."

I felt fire ignite inside me and I reached for it, brushing lightly against the searing heat. "You will never have me, or Camelot. The Dark has no place in this world."

My fist collided with the ground, the impact jarring up my arm. Shock waves splintered the surrounding ground, radiating out in a wave towards the startled demons. Liquid fire poured out of the fissures like tentacles, wrapping around the creature's ankles. Magma consumed them in a matter of seconds and they exploded into ash.

I brushed off my filthy hands on my trousers and huffed. "Take that, arseholes."

Scrambling back up the hill, I rejoined the dwindling battle. The Dark had lost significant numbers, but many Naturals had also fallen. My heart twisted and I looked to the sky.

The black cloud of Ikakantor's soul was still heaving, controlling the remaining demons. I had to stop this before more Naturals died.

I gauged the distance between me and Ikakantor's demonic essence. Could I make it?

"Madeleine!"

Twenty metres away, Trent had spotted me watching the sky. I nodded.

He knelt on the ground and slapped his shoulders. Without a second thought, I sprinted towards him and leapt. My boots landed on his shoulders, my hand wrapped around the hilt of his arondight blade, and he jumped, launching me into the into the air with a burst of Light.

The arondight blade flashed as I rushed towards Ikakantor's essence, wind whipping past my cheeks. The cloud sparked with menacing snaps of electricity and I raised the sword above my head. I swung, slicing through the centre of the angry storm of Darkness.

Ikakantor parted with a screech that tore at my eardrums and I twisted in the air, watching him split as I hurtled back to Earth.

I landed, the force sending me to my knees and the heels of my boots digging into the soft earth.

The cracking Darkness twisted together, spinning like a tornado, a shriek tearing through the air and echoing across the valley like the wail of a banshee.

Trent skidded to a stop beside me, wheezing.

"Is he dying?" he asked.

"Wounded, I think," I replied, handing him back his sword.

"Shite. I thought you'd be able to kill him."

I shrugged. "If I'm able to, I don't know how…"

The remaining demons wailed as Ikakantor shot through the sky and disappeared over the ridge. The creatures began to sprint after him, but a wave of Naturals chased them down, sending them back to oblivion.

I stilled, my heart galloping in my chest, and took a breath. I was covered in soot and demon blood, and my hair was tangled with much of the same goop. My face was likely as filthy as my hands, too.

The remains of two hundred demons fluttered into the air, twisting and turning like a flurry of snow in the aftermath of a blizzard. If I didn't know what they were, the sight of the soft flakes would have been beautiful, but the destruction that had torn the hillside apart was a stark reminder.

Weariness seeped into my bones as I swept my gaze across the surviving Naturals. Spotting Maisy, who was covered in blood and grime, I rushed towards her with Trent on my heels.

"Maisy."

"I'm okay." She waved us off and gestured to herself. "This is all demon goop."

"You fought like a mad woman," Trent told her.

She flushed, her cheeks reddening as she wiped at the soot smeared across them. "Let's face it. That was terrifying."

Trent snorted and hugged her. "Honestly, I pissed my pants a little."

I blinked as Issac emerged through the swirling ash, walking towards us, his arondight hilt in his hand.

"So, you can fight after all," I said as he stood before me.

"Madeleine." He placed a hand on my shoulder, his Light fluttering against my power. If he was concerned I was going to have a meltdown and turn Camelot into a volcano, he had nothing to worry about.

"Where's Greer?" I asked.

"Right here." The acting Inquisitor leaned against the crushed remains of the lead car in the convoy and grimaced.

"Are you all right?" Issac offered her his arm, which she gladly took.

"As protector of the Codex, they're connected to me," she murmured. "I can feel every loss."

The battle must have been difficult for her, even though it had barely lasted fifteen minutes. Naturals had given their lives for Camelot and each soul had torn at her own as they left our world for the next.

But now I understood why she'd ruled for me to return to Camelot. I was still a Natural, even though it was only a part of what I was becoming. She knew I had potential to remain with the Light.

"We must return to the safety of Camelot," she continued, raising her voice. "Everyone who is able, assist the wounded and bring the fallen back to camp."

Trent and Maisy moved off to assist and I took a step towards the field, but Greer called out to me.

"Madeleine." She glanced at Issac, who nodded.

Eilhana. The memory of the power the name had over me was a barbed echo.

"You heard," I said. "My…true name. Ikakantor baited me with it the night I faced him on the ridge, but I didn't believe him."

"You had no reason to," Greer said.

"It's a problem." I looked at Issac.

"A problem that we'll figure out," he said, "*together.*"

"It must not be uttered," Greer ordered. "We are the only three besides Ikakantor who know it."

"I will take the secret to my grave if I have to," Issac told me.

I stared at him, hardly wanting to believe him. Ash clung to his clothes and dusted through his dishevelled hair, the grime making his eyes shine a brilliant emerald. My breath hitched and whatever I was going to say caught in my throat.

"Come," he said, covering my awkward silence, "let's get back to the city."

I didn't have any other choice. Trust had to go both ways now.

As the Naturals staggered towards Camelot, I looked over my shoulder and grimaced. The hillside looked like another planet—an echo of the ruined worlds the Dark had left in their wake before reaching ours.

I prayed it wasn't an omen.

11

———

Camelot remained on high alert throughout the night and the next day.

I'd recovered quickly, the strange power had all but patched me up better than my Light could have on its own, but the mood in the camp was an odd mix of elation and sadness.

Five warriors had fallen on the field. Greer said it was a miracle more lives weren't lost considering the odds, but I'd taken out a large portion of the Dark before they'd even crossed swords with the Naturals.

If anyone asked me, it was cold comfort.

Aiden had mapped out a section of the city where there used to be a cemetery. Here there were a mixture of mausoleums and below ground burials—the former not customarily seen in England during the Middle Ages. It gave the walled area a gloomy feel.

The entire population of modern-day Camelot had assembled here—apart from those guarding the walls—to bid farewell to the lives lost in yesterday's battle.

Until now, the Naturals had interred their fallen at a separate site at Glastonbury. The infamous location also housed our prison in the catacombs under the Tor, but it had been a site heavily used by the Druids before it was overrun by the Dark and much of their power lingered to this day. The Naturals owed a great deal to them.

I stood at the back of the assembled crowd, watching as the coffins of all five warriors were positioned beside their resting places. Their families considered it a great honour for their loved ones to be amongst the first buried in Camelot since the cataclysm. For me, even though we all knew what we risked, their deaths were hard to reconcile.

Greer was speaking, but her words slipped past me without registering. My head was filled with ash, smoke, and fire. Issac stood beside her, his head lowered.

Trent nudged me. "Are you all right?"

I nodded and focused on Greer.

"Yesterday, Camelot saw the greatest battle the Naturals have fought since the assault on Brent Castle. The day the rift closed, the last bastion of our people stood against the full force of the Dark as the Twin Flames descended into the portal at the centre of the castle." She gestured towards the rise where the remains of the fortress towered above us. "The same castle we fought to defend yesterday."

Five Naturals stepped forwards and covered each

coffin with a flag bearing the Pendragon coat of arms —three golden crowns on a field of rich, royal blue. It was the only symbol we had left of the Naturals before the cataclysm and it had come to represent more than just Wilder and Arthur's bloodline. It was Camelot. It was all Naturals.

"They gave their lives for the balance," Greer continued. "They gave their lives to protect the living. For the Light."

"*For the Light*," the crowd echoed.

"May they never be forgotten." She raised her hands and golden Light bloomed in her palms.

Then everyone raised their hands, adding to the gold hue until the cemetery was aglow. I stepped back and shoved my hands into my pockets. Raising demonic-tinted Light felt like it would be an insult rather than a show of solidarity.

Silence fell over the city as they lowered the coffins into the earth, and when they'd settled, the Light was extinguished.

The funeral was over and the Naturals began to break away, returning to their posts. Trent offered me a reassuring smile as he joined them, leaving me to my thoughts.

Caleb Thompson walked past me, throwing me a look that would wither even the strongest warrior. Clearly, he still didn't trust me. *What a surprise.*

"That was some glare," Issac said, appearing beside me.

"Thompson and I have history," I explained. "Mostly it's because of me being a pain in his arse and undermining his authority. We just keep away from one another now."

"Just a normal day, then."

I grunted and lowered my gaze as the crowd began to disperse.

"You did a great thing yesterday," he murmured. "Without your help, I'm not sure we would've won without losing more people."

After all the hate I'd endured, being a hero was a foreign concept, and I wasn't sure I fit the role. Rhys was laying in the infirmary—and others who held the same ideology—and was on the way to making a full recovery. I wasn't sure how he was going to take it, knowing that I saved him from being disembowelled.

"Well," he said, smiling, "you got your moment of redemption."

This *was* my moment. I'd dreamed about being accepted by my own people ever since the day at the Academy when Scarlett saved my soul. But I'd never fit in to begin with…

After my performance, I didn't know who or what I identified as anymore.

"Did I?" I shook my head. "That hill was a lovely picnic spot before I got to it."

Issac chuckled. "In all seriousness, you proved your intentions to Camelot and the Regula. Now, no one can doubt who you fight for and really, who's going to challenge you?"

I smirked and turned back to the procession as it wound its way through the streets. "I just wish I could have saved them all…"

"Saving Camelot isn't just up to you."

"If Scarlett and Wilder were here, the Dark would never have attacked like that."

Issac frowned. "Whatever's in that vault must be worth dying for."

"I don't want to know what it is. I'd rather the leak was plugged. Maybe then the Flames would wake up."

"Perhaps, but there's still so much we don't know."

He was right, No one understood where the Lady of the Lake had come from, let alone what she was. According to Scarlett, she'd called herself a celestial being, and in turn, we'd dubbed her a Celestial—whatever that meant. All it did was conjure images of grey aliens and spaceships to me. Somehow, I couldn't see interstellar travel in a flying saucer as being a part of the story.

"Why did Ikakantor think it was a good idea to attack?" I wondered. "He must've known it was suicide."

"It was a test," Issac replied. "He was trying to find our weakness. His body can be replaced and those demons were just fodder."

"There can't be all that many left to throw away on a suicide mission."

"Which means what they want is worth dying for."

I stilled. "The vault is their last resort."

"If it's truly the vault they want…"

"Ikakantor compelled the entire city to dig up the archive," I argued. "If it's not the vault, it's something inside the archive at least…but I still think it's the vault. I can feel the energy inside it."

We fell into silence as the last of the Naturals left the cemetery.

Once we were alone, Issac peered at me. "The collar was never going to work, was it?"

"No," I replied.

"Then I guess we're even."

"I guess so."

We walked together, leaving the fallen to their slumber, and returned to base camp.

As we entered the first row of tents, Issac gestured for me to stop. "I think someone wants to speak to you."

I followed his gaze and saw my mother rushing to meet us. Issac raised his eyebrows and retreated, leaving us in private.

"Mum."

"There you are," she said, pulling me in for a hug. "I was so worried. You disappeared after the battle."

"I thought it was for the best."

She drew back. "Why would you think that?"

"You saw the destruction I caused."

Mum smiled and brushed my hair behind my ears. "You saved Camelot yesterday. You saved Greer."

My bottom lip trembled. "But at what cost?"

"Madeleine, you have a warrior's cunning, but your heart is full of Light. We are Naturals and we do what we have to protect the Earth." She grimaced and added, "And humanity, despite its failings."

I laughed, my mother's words breaking through my melancholy. Her loathing for humanity's treatment of the environment was legendary. I didn't know how many rants about CO2 and single-use plastic I'd sat through as a child. "Please tell me you're working on reducing carbon emissions."

"*I wish*. The Industrial Revolution was the worst thing that ever happened to this planet. Besides the Dark, that is."

"Mum…" my smile faded, "do you hate me?"

Her shoulders sank and she studied my features for a long moment. "We've never been close, have we?"

I shook my head.

"I'm sorry, Madeleine. Your father and I have always prioritised work. Even when…even when you were sick…" she trailed off with a sigh. Bethany Greenbriar was many things, but maternal had never quite made the list. "It doesn't matter what you are, only who you choose to be. The power you commanded yesterday was terrifying, and that's the truth."

I grunted and lowered my gaze. *Way to state the obvious, Mum.*

"*But* you used it in defence of the Light." She took my hands in hers. "Madeleine, no matter what you become, you'll always be our daughter. I could never hate you. *Ever*."

She embraced me and I pressed my cheek against her heart, swallowing my tears before they spilled.

"You didn't choose to become this," she whispered

against my hair. "After yesterday, I think you might be the only one who can save us."

I picked up on the sorrowful note in her voice. "You're leaving again, aren't you?"

"I have to."

I withdrew from her arms and nodded. "I understand."

"The work your father and I are doing is important. If we're successful, it could help with Camelot's defences."

"I know," I told her. "I just wish I could help. Being unpredictable has its drawbacks."

"I believe in you, Madeleine. You are a Greenbriar, after all."

I smiled, more for her benefit than mine. At least now I knew what I was capable of.

And that had to mean something.

I walked into the mess tent that night to a riotous round of applause that had me blushing. It was an epic whiplash moment after the hostility I'd felt when I'd first arrived at Camelot.

"Madeleine!"

I followed the sound of Trent's voice and found him and Maisy at a table in the back. It was lucky they'd found a place to sit—it was standing room only tonight.

"You're a celebrity now," Maisy said as I slipped into a chair beside her. "How does it feel?"

"*Surreal.*"

Amanda joined us and set a tray of food in front of me. "I didn't think you'd get there and back before it got cold so I got you a bit of everything."

"Thanks." My cheeks flared and it was a wonder I didn't burst into flames like that hillside.

"You were right…" Trent said. "About us being complacent."

"It doesn't matter," I told him. "We're all on the same page now."

"We should have—"

I kicked him under the table. "*Should haves* won't get us anywhere. *What's nexts* will."

"She's a philosopher, too," Maisy said with a laugh.

"Stop it," I muttered, shrinking in on myself. It was my favourite go-to tactic from my teenage years when Kayla, the queen antagoniser, was circling.

"Sit up!" Trent exclaimed, pressing his palm against my back to straighten my spine. "You're a hero, Mads. Soak it up while you can."

"I don't like the spotlight," I told them. "I just did what I had to."

"You ran across that field and faced those demons on your own," Amanda said. "I didn't see it, but can you imagine…?"

"It was bad arse," Maisy declared. "Then she just raised her arms and *POW!*"

"That lava was so cool."

I shook my head, embarrassed at all the attention. It may seem incredible, but the burden of what my soul had evolved into wasn't something I thought we should celebrate. No one should have absolute power. I still had a human heart, and I could be corrupted just as easily as everyone in this room. Aiden had taught us all about the dangers of too much of a good thing in our history and ethics classes at the Academy.

The Lady of the Lake had granted Arthur and Lancelot the greatest power the world had ever seen, and they'd crossed their swords—Arondight and Excalibur—with hate in their hearts. Ripping a hole in space and time was one thing but turning the planet into an ocean of lava seemed like a real possibility from where I was standing.

"You look worried," Maisy said, breaking me out of my downward thought spiral.

I shrugged. "I am. You all saw what I did. There has to be a point where it all comes unstuck."

"Unstuck how?" she asked.

"Nature always finds a loophole."

Trent snorted. "You're unstoppable, Mads. You tore up that hill with a flick of your wrist."

"Yeah, Madeleine's right," Amanda said. "The balance always finds a way to curb ultimate power. Look at the Flames. With Arondight and Excalibur leading us, we were unstoppable."

"But they have a weakness," Trent mused.

"Everything does," I said with a sigh. "That's the point. Natural Light is limited and even the Druid's power was finite." My weakness was the name Ikakantor had spoken. *Eilhana.*

I carried the greater demon's Darkness in my soul,

and now I shared the burden of her true name. I didn't know what was stranger—the name or that demons identified as male and female. It seemed like a rather human concept if you asked me.

They had made me from Eilhana and Mordred. Knowing what the latter could do, I shuddered at the thought. Mordred could shift his body into a creature made of smoke and bone—and his Darkness had been enough to stand against the Twin Flames.

"Oh, enough of that," Amanda declared. "We'll have enough time to worry about reprisals in the morning. Tonight, we're honouring the fallen and the fact that we're still alive. This is tradition, Madeleine. No pouting allowed."

Trent grinned and stood so abruptly that his chair fell onto the floor behind him. "Three cheers for Madeleine, the lava goddess!"

The mess tent erupted in a wave of cheers and I covered my face, wishing some molten earth would rise up and swallow me whole.

That night, I was welcomed back into the barracks and treated to the childish game known as 'the floor is lava'. Whenever someone yelled it, everyone had five seconds to get to higher ground. It resulted in hysterics, and someone fell off a chair every single time.

After the last two days, I let them have their fun— it was the calm before the storm, after all.

12

———

The following morning, Issac and I returned to the jousting field to train.

We both had a lot on our minds after the battle and neither of us seemed to know how to begin. For once, Issac was lost for inspiration. He seemed like the kind of guy who drafted lesson plans the night before class, but no one had seen my bothersome true name coming, least of all me.

I thought Ikakantor had been lying. I shook my head, the movement stirring Issac to life.

"I don't think you realise how you looked when you fought, Madeleine."

I groaned. "I didn't have that freaky red eye vein thing again, did I?"

"You were too far away to see."

I snorted and sat on the bottom row of the stone bleachers. "I probably looked like a demon on acid for all I know."

"That fire you called…" Issac lowered his gaze and frowned.

I straightened up, a little worried he was reverting to his skeptical ways. "What?"

"Well, it seems less demonic and more… I don't know."

"More what?"

"Druidic."

I scoffed and shook my head. Being both Light and Dark was more than enough. To throw the possibility of a third supernatural race into the pot? Unthinkable.

"Impossible," I told him. "We've seen demons use fire in their Darkness before. They can manipulate regular elemental flame while Naturals have to create their own. That's all it was. I brought forth the lava that was already in the ground."

"We don't understand what or who this greater demon used in her experiments. The Druids were hunted and many of them were killed. This was going on at the same time Mordred was taken from Guinevere and experimented on. It's possible—"

"The Druids left like eight hundred years ago. Like we remember anything accurate about their powers anyway." I shook my head, thinking of Elijah. He'd known, but he never admitted to me what he was. I only suspected him being a Druid.

"You read Scarlett's report," Issac said, sitting beside me. "She went back in time and saw them. She rode with the Druidess Gilhana."

"A *glimpse*."

"A Druidess who *burned down* Glastonbury by raising her *arms*…then turned into a hawk."

"I don't need the added pressure. I'm supposed to be a Natural and that's it."

Issac grunted, annoyed at my constant arguing. I knew what he believed, but it wasn't that simple. I couldn't be everything all at the same time. Not even Excalibur and Arondight could contain the melting pot of heritage and not spontaneously combust.

"Can we talk about something else?" I asked. "There's more pressing matters, don't you think?"

He leaned forwards, pressing his elbows on his knees. "Your true name."

"How could I even have one? I don't understand. I only have a little demon in me."

"We know very little about them," Issac replied. "If the Druids were still with us, perhaps they would know."

I thought about Elijah again, but that was a pipe dream. "Maybe there's something in the archive?"

"Perhaps…but finding it may take years."

"Mordred must have been made from the same greater demon," I mused. "Would all hybrids have the same true name, then?" I scratched my head, wondering if Elijah had the same problem. Maybe that's why Ikakantor could bind him. He had a name as a byproduct of the demon he was created from and his Druidic name. *Theoretically.*

"Maybe, but thankfully there aren't any more." He glanced at me out the corner of his eye. None like we knew from the experiments of Human

Convergence at least. "No, I don't think it's that simple."

"It's because the mutation fused with my soul, right?"

"That's the most logical conclusion."

I looked across the jousting field and imagined armoured knights galloping on majestic horses, shattering lances, and the clash of metal as they tumbled to the ground. I bet Arthur Pendragon didn't have these kinds of problems, but eight hundred years trapped in a twisted reality as a slave to the Dark was a whole other kettle of fish.

No, my problems weren't any worse or better off than anyone else's. At least mine came with new superpowers that could help my friends.

"How do you suppose I might fight back against this true name business?" I asked. "Ikakantor just said it and I was like a useless bag of bones."

"What was it like?" Issac murmured.

"I could feel the power in it," I replied, wringing my hands together. "Each syllable sucked the energy out of my body like a bullet tearing through my flesh. It hurt…big time."

"It's a major problem. You have to learn how to separate that part of yourself."

"How?"

"Meditation and spiritual awareness."

I smirked. "You're the man for the job, huh? How convenient."

"Much of who we are is spiritual, Madeleine," he explained. "Our powers are linked to our souls, not our bodies. This," he held up his hands, "is just flesh and bone. A tool to manifest our spirit."

"That's deep." I stared at his palms and decided they were far too smooth to wield a blade as well as he had the day of the battle. He had though and surprised me in the process.

"The mind is a powerful thing."

I already knew that. My beliefs—and my secret wants—had caught me out a few times already. Issac was the expert.

"So, if I believe it has no power over me, it won't?" I wondered out loud.

Issac nodded. "You can nullify Light, why not this?"

"Nullifying powers, altering memories, walking in other people's subconscious minds, tearing apart the Earth… Where does it all end?"

"Maybe that's it."

"Maybe."

"Madeleine…can I show you something?"

He took my hands in his and I hesitated. His touch was gentle and not appropriate for our teacher/student relationship.

"So, you like me now?" I asked, attempting to hide my embarrassment. "You aren't afraid I'll get into your head again?"

"As if you could," he said with a smirk. He ran his thumbs over my knuckles, and I was suddenly conflicted.

"Show me what?" I whispered.

"An explanation, I guess."

I felt his Light brush against mine. Hesitating, I went to pull away.

"Trust me," Issac said as he tightened his grip.

"Trust you? I'm more worried about you trusting me."

He smiled and let his Light wind around mine, drawing me into his memories.

I blinked and the jousting field blurred. I blinked again and we stood on a path beside a fast-flowing river.

It was much wider than the Thames—boats and water taxis bobbed up and along the choppy current, passing underneath several bridges that dwarfed even Tower Bridge in London. Above, buildings filled the skyline and I gasped. I recognised the Empire State Building towering above the rest, even though I'd never seen it in person.

"Is this…?"

"New York." Issac pointed towards the water. "That's the East River. The Sanctum is not far. It's on Roosevelt Island, though there are smaller outposts and safe houses throughout Manhattan."

I looked out over the urban sprawl, wondering what it must look like all lit up at night. "I never knew it was so big."

"The island isn't that large," Issac told me. "But humans have crammed a lot of stuff onto it over the years. I used to stand here and wonder how it all didn't sink into the ocean, but once you're inside the city, its size becomes irrelevant." He took my hand again and the vision changed.

This time we stood in the foyer of a grand mansion but it had been torn apart. The floorboards still smoked with hidden embers and the air had the rotten egg stench that was a marker for demonic activity. The roof had been torn open and the sky shone blue through the massive hole.

"This is the New York Sanctum?" I asked.

"It's not as grand as London's, but it's got enough history of its own to fill another Codex," Issac told me. "I came here with my family when I was sixteen. My parents were stationed here while my sister and I went to the academy in Brooklyn."

"I thought you went to some fancy human school?" I asked.

"I went to Harvard after I graduated. Human psychology isn't all that different."

"Apart from the magical powers."

"Yes, well, there is *that*."

I stepped over a fallen beam and looked up through the hole in the ceiling. Whatever had impacted the old mansion had smashed through four stories and into the basement below.

Issac's boots crunched on the debris underfoot. "This was all that was left after the Dark Night attacks."

"What hit the roof?" I wondered.

"You don't want to know…" he replied wryly. "I was in the east wing with my family that night. The explosion took us all off guard and by the time the alarms sounded, they were already inside."

I remembered now. New York was one of the

hardest hit. London had been bad, but it had been much worse here.

"They killed my father first," he murmured. "He pushed us back and faced them head-on. Then my mother died." His voice broke and he lowered his gaze. "Another explosion rocked the mansion and the floor came apart underneath us. She slipped from my arms, but I caught her. There were… On the floor below, I could see demons rushing past and she was hanging. She was… They grabbed her and…her hand was still in mine, but she was gone."

He'd lost his entire family and now he was alone. It was no wonder why he had hated me. I represented everything he loathed.

"I'm sorry I said those things about you," he said.

"They came from a place of suffering. I understand now that it wasn't personal."

"I couldn't separate my past from you as a person. I—"

I covered his mouth with my hand. "Issac? Shut the hell up."

He curled his fingers around my wrist and tugged. We were closer than I realised and I tensed.

"Madeleine, I—"

"I'm worried," I interrupted. "The power I felt… It was consuming. *Intoxicating*." My gaze searched his. "What if I lose myself in it?"

"You won't," he replied. "If it was going to take you, it would have already."

"For someone who loathed what I was a few short weeks ago, you sure have a lot of faith in me."

"I see who you are now," he whispered. "Your strength, your determination…"

A zap of electricity pulsed through my body as I realised we were in the kissing zone and I lowered my gaze. I wasn't sure if I wanted to go there. Our training was intimate, but romantically? Men made me nervous when they looked at me the way Issac was looking at me right now.

I was good at sabotage, so I blurted, "If I ever find Elijah, would you consider… Would you consider helping him?"

Issac frowned as the vision of New York faded around us. "Why are you still protecting him?"

"He's not our enemy. He's a victim. If we have the power to help him, shouldn't we?"

He fell silent, his gaze piercing mine.

The wind had risen while we were in his memory, and I shivered. There was ice in the air, and it wasn't just the approaching winter.

"We're finished for today," he said, letting my hands go.

"Issac?"

"Masters has requested your assistance with his barrier," he told me. "You should make your way up to the archive."

"But—"

"I'll continue to work on your true name," he interrupted. "Greer has been consulting the Codex."

"You should have led with that," I drawled.

"Among other things…" he said, ever the cryptic.

I descended into the archive with a heavy heart. The smell of musty parchment and uncirculated air wasn't doing anything to make me feel better.

Confused had nothing on my mood. My life was filled with more questions and mysteries than answers and understanding.

Did Issac… Did he *like* me? Did I like him? For the first time in my entire life, I wish I understood romance, but I had bigger problems than which guy I wanted to kiss.

The vault hadn't changed one bit as I approached it. Masters had a table and chair set up before the decorative doors, with two large balls of Light illuminating the entire length of the hall.

The rest of the space wasn't as grand as the vault itself. The walls bore no markings—not even a mural or a rune marked the stone.

"Ah, Madeleine," Masters said, brushing off his hands, "there you are."

I looked up at the vault door and my stomach gurgled. "You asked for me?"

"Yes, yes of course. I've spent two weeks weaving this barrier," he explained. "This is my best work, but I don't know if it's enough."

I studied the golden Light radiating amongst the cogs and gears. The web was intricate and layered, each strand following the curves of the lock and even the decorative carvings. No part of the door was left bare—even the hinges and surrounding walls were coated.

"I'm not sure what you want me to do," I said. "I can nullify this and walk straight into that vault…if the door was open."

"Would you destroy it?" he asked. "I mean, if you walked through the barrier, would it dissolve?"

"I don't think so. It hasn't the few times I've tried."

He gestured at the vault. "Touch it."

I hesitated. "Touch the door that's making the Flames sick?"

"Sure."

Shrugging, I pressed my palm against the door. Master's Light barrier tingled against my skin and a pulse of the foreign energy leaking from the vault sighed through my body.

I pulled back, confused.

"What is it?" Masters asked, standing beside me.

"A sigh."

"A sigh?" Masters scratched his head. "Well, that's strange." He picked up his notebook and began to flip through the pages. I frowned at the notes and drawings he'd scribbled down and wondered when he'd last slept. "Are you still feeling nauseous?"

"Not as much as before."

"But still a little? Interesting." He scribbled something in his notebook. "Do you think you could help me weave a web? I'm thinking your abilities might seal this energy spike for good."

"I'm not sure I remember much about this kind of Light," I said. "But I can try."

"I'm going to have to consult with Issac of course, but I don't see why it wouldn't work. Leave it with me."

"Okay well, I'm going back upstairs to help Aiden with the cataloguing."

I left Masters to his own devices and returned to the foyer where Aiden was sitting at a folding table, peering at a crusty book through a magnifying glass.

"Hey."

Looking up from his work, he said, "Masters was looking for you."

"I just saw him."

"You did? Great."

"He seems a little… Well, when was the last time he saw sunlight?"

"It's hard to say," Aiden replied. "His work is important, and he lives and breathes the mastering of Light. Masters is good at what he does, but he can be a little obsessive."

"He wants me to use my abilities."

"Well, it's the only thing we haven't tried. I know you worry about controlling them, but we're trying to wake the Flames from their coma."

"I know. He wants to consult with Issac first, but the more I think about it, the more I wonder with my powers being all weird that any web I might be able to weave might just undo all his work."

Aiden smiled in an attempt to reassure me. "We'll

figure it out. Issac will know your limits and we can test them out in the city before tackling the vault."

He leaned over the magnifying glass again, signalling I was dismissed.

I sought out Amanda and we worked together on a new shelf of ancient tax ledgers until it was time to head back to base camp for dinner. After my action-packed day, I wasn't in the mood for the noise and chaos of mealtime, so instead, I lingered in the archive.

I had an ulterior motive, though. With no one looking over my shoulder, I could search the foyer for any clues about my true name. It was probably a long shot, but the next time Ikakantor came knocking, I had to be ready.

The archive was a little creepy with no one in it. The shelves cast long shadows and knowing there were unexplored depths in the hallways beyond made me shiver. Then there was the portal Craig had found behind the door across the room. It could lead anywhere.

I snorted and returned to the shelves, scanning titles and flipping open covers. I'd fought an army of demons single-handedly and here I was, creeped out by a portal? *Whatever.*

"Watchya lookin' for?"

I jumped, my heart skipping several beats, and swore. A pair of emerald green eyes stared at me through a space in the bookshelf and I shoved a pile of priceless—and fragile—books aside.

A familiar, roguish face grinned at me and I was stuck between elation and terror. "Elijah?"

He grinned and wiggled his eyebrows up and down. "Miss me?"

"What the hell are you doing here? How—"

"You should really lock that thing up," he said, nodding towards the portal. The door was open, revealing the oily surface of the wormhole that lead to who knew where.

"You came through the—" I stamped my foot. "*Elijah.*"

"Better me than your BFF Ikakantor. Who, by the way, is still floating around as an angry little thundercloud. He can barley hold himself together. Seems someone cut him in half with a sparkly sword."

"He deserved it." I narrowed my eyes as he rounded the end of the shelf.

Elijah laughed and raked his gaze over me. He licked his lips and grinned like he'd just won the jackpot. I knew his Dark side was in control, and he was handsome as he was sweet, but his demon gave him an epic creep factor.

"How did you…?" I stared at the portal. He must know where the other end went.

"The door was locked and someone opened it."

"*Duh.*"

"Be careful who you're calling stupid, pretty spectre. Someone broke the lock and now things can go both ways." He tapped the doorframe. "Sometimes things are the way they are for a reason."

"Where does it go?"

"Why? Do you want to see?"

"No, I—"

Before I could finish arguing, Elijah smirked and pulled me through the portal, our destination unknown.

13

———

I fell through the portal, the glassy surface tearing the scream from my lips.

There was a burst of complete darkness before light erupted around us. I landed on my hands and knees, and mud squelched between my fingers and seeped into my boots. Elijah fared much better—he landed on his feet like he was on a leisurely stroll in the park.

I wiped my palms on my shirt and looked up, blinking as a drop of water slapped me in the face.

Impossibly tall trees towered over us, their tops covering the sky like enormous green umbrellas. Shafts of light streamed through gaps in the foliage, coating the forest with dappled spots.

Everywhere I looked was green—vines, trees, bushes, moss, ferns. I'm sure they all had names, but I was too stunned to pick any out. We were so far from the lonely hills of Camelot, it wasn't funny.

I stilled as the strange sounds of exotic bird calls

whistled through the thick air. The heat was heavy like a steaming wet blanket had been thrown around my shoulders. It smelt like damp earth and fresh rain.

Elijah stood over me, watching my assessment with a curious expression. His hair had grown out some, and it was looking more shaggy than shaved. His Scottish accent seemed thicker somehow, and his demonic side… well, let's just say he'd taken me to a rainforest and dumped me in the mud against my will.

"Where are we?" I asked.

"A rainforest," he replied, helping me out of the mud.

"I can see that," I exclaimed, gesturing to the glossy greenery.

"It's the perfect place for a demon, don't you think? It's full of dangerous creatures. Have you met the snake people?"

I scowled. "Snake people?"

"Snake *shifters*." Elijah rolled his eyes. "If you think you'll have nothing left to fight once the Dark is gone, think again. This world is full of supernatural creatures just waiting to eat juicy women like you."

"Elijah, just tell me where we are in the world."

"Borneo."

"We're in Indonesia?" I sighed and threw my hands into the air. "Great. Just *great*."

His lips curved upwards. "Do you want to see my lean-to?"

"I want to go back to Camelot," I replied. "I'm on probation after all those stupid stunts we pulled, or have you forgotten?"

"I never forget a good time." He smirked and wiggled his eyebrows.

I hissed at him and turned to the portal, but I saw nothing but dense jungle.

"Where did it go?" I demanded, trying not to panic. "Please don't tell me it's one-way."

"If it's one-way, how do you think I got into your crusty archive?"

"Who cares?" I exclaimed. "I just need to go back!" Camelot had been attacked only three days ago. Anyone with a brain knew now was the best time to counterstrike. Ikakantor had a whole closet of meat suits, which meant he could be back at any time. *Any. Time.*

Elijah sighed and leaned against a tree. "Not yet. We have to wait for the portal to swing back around."

"*Wait.* It's on a timer? I didn't know that was a thing."

He stared at me like I was a few sandwiches short of a picnic. "It's a thing."

"Anything could find it. Camelot is totally open to the Dark. I have to go back and warn the others."

"They'll be fine." He began to pick at his fingernails. "This portal has been active for hundreds of years. If the Dark was going to find it, they would have already. Besides, until some dolt opened the door, it was a one-way trip to nowhere."

"But—"

"Let me clear this up for you. The Dark doesn't know how to create portals, let alone find them," Elijah said with a roll of his eyes. "If they did, they wouldn't have needed your rift to cross into this world, or any world for that matter."

"Then how did they consume so many?"

"They had help, *duh*."

"From who?"

He shrugged. "Whoever they were, they aren't here anymore."

"Then how do you know how to use it?"

He wiggled his fingers at me and whispered, "*Magic*."

"I suppose that's why they liked you so much, because I can see it wasn't for your charisma." I pursed my lips and shrugged off my jacket, the humidity of the jungle getting to me. Even with my Light staving off the heat, the air was still thick with moisture.

"As much as I love arguing with you, it's going to rain in a minute. I'd rather be inside when it does."

"How do you know that?"

"My demon senses are tingling. They don't like to get wet."

"Why, will you melt?"

Elijah rolled his eyes and began to walk off through the forest, leaving me no choice but to follow.

"Why did you bring me here?" I demanded.

He shrugged. "Maybe I missed you."

"You missed me?" I scoffed. I missed him too, but this was a little much.

"You better tuck your trousers into your boots," he threw over his shoulder. "You don't want anything crawling up those pretty legs of yours."

I yelped and swatted at my legs, quickly shoving my trouser bottoms into the top of my combat boots.

It was a short walk through thick jungle, but the trek was cumbersome and thoroughly annoying. Everywhere I turned, vines or some other irritating vegetation seemed to block our path. Elijah swept aside branches so I could duck underneath, but I wished I had a machete to hack away the aggressive growth.

If that wasn't an ironic metaphor for my life, I didn't know what was.

"Here we are."

I glanced up, expecting a hovel with leave blankets and a hole for a toilet, but I was pleasantly surprised to find an actual house.

It looked like three forty-foot shipping containers had been polished and renovated into a posh eco-lodge designed to blend in with the surrounding rainforest. There was even a graded driveway with a four-wheel drive parked in an undercover carport, but I couldn't spot where the front door was until Elijah led me around the side of the property.

"When you said lean-to, I was expecting a branch and some palm fronds," I said as we stepped up onto the small deck.

He laughed and opened the door. "Some rich human tosser lived here. He said it was his *holiday home*." He snorted and ushered me inside. "It's eco-friendly and self-sufficient. Totally off-grid. I needed it more than his soft arse did."

I narrowed my eyes. "What did you do to him?"

"I didn't kill him if that's what you're getting your knickers all twisted about. I sent him off looking for the local orangutan colony. If he wants to save something, he can save critically endangered, furry ginger primates. All he was going to do was sit in here and binge watch the latest season of whatever on Netflix."

"I highly doubt there's internet access out here."

"That's what you took from all of that? How's the WiFi?" It was his turn to throw his hands into the air. "I'm trying to win your love by showing how benevolent I can be even when I'm Dark."

I ignored him. Checking out the house, I found a small kitchen, dining room, bedrooms, and a modern bathroom. Everything was in spitting distance, so it didn't take much effort to memorise the layout. It was furnished with a minimal design in mind, so there weren't any knick-knacks on the reclaimed wooden coffee table or paintings on the walls. The couch looked rather soft and inviting, though.

A floor-to-ceiling glass panel took up one entire wall of the lounge room, letting in swathes of natural light. It overlooked the forest and there was even a space that opened out to the sky. The house must be on a rise high enough to break through the canopy at least a little.

From here, the jungle didn't seem so dangerous. It just stretched out as far as the eye could see. It was beautiful in a deadly kind of way, which made it perfect for someone like Elijah.

"I heard you turned that delightful hill outside of

Camelot into magma," Elijah's voice echoed behind me.

I turned. "So?"

His eyes sparkled and I sensed his Darkness stirring. "Destruction feels nice, doesn't it?"

"Don't make it out to be anything Dark, Elijah," I snapped. "I know your arsehole switch is stuck in the on position, but don't tempt me."

"Tempt you?" He laughed and raked his gaze over me. "To do what, I wonder?"

"To go to the Dark."

"There are some benefits," he told me, "like fire… I hear you like fire."

I sighed, already exasperated. "You could be the wise mentor of this story, yet you're only interested in insulting me."

"I don't know how you came to that conclusion," he huffed. "I'm complimenting you."

"You're nothing but trouble!"

"*I'm* trouble? You're the real deal, pretty spectre. You're the queen of a good time."

"You're the one who snatched me from Camelot," I reminded him. "You just appeared out of thin air and dragged me through that portal. Why? And because you missed me isn't the answer I'm looking for."

Elijah grasped my face in his hands and kissed me, the abrupt movement taking my breath away. When he drew back, he did so with regretful purpose. He wanted more, but there must be some shred of his former self still hanging on to make him hesitate.

"*I missed you*," he whispered. "I don't want us to be apart. I want you to be with me always."

"Elijah, I can't leave Camelot. The Naturals need my help. Wilder and Scarlett…they saved my Light. And Scarlett… She saved my soul from being erased. I owe them, but it's not just that."

"You love them," he said slowly. "I know how that feels."

I sucked in a shaky breath. "This doesn't have to be how it is for us."

He clutched me in a vice grip, his whole body trembling.

"You gave up your humanity to save me," I murmured. "Let me return the favour."

"Can't we just stay here?" he whispered. "I can introduce you to the snake people."

I pulled back with a sigh. "Elijah, I'm serious."

"So am I. They'll want to eat you, but I can convince them that you taste nasty."

"*Light help me*," I muttered.

"Once they get over the fact that they can't swallow you whole, they're really nice."

His evasiveness was starting to get to me. He always withheld things, but our situation had become more dire. Elijah could help us if he was just straight with me about who he was, and vice versa, but he was too busy hiding out in a secluded rainforest to care.

"Are you still linked to Ikakantor?" He opened his mouth and I added, "I want the truth, Elijah."

He shook his head. "When I gave up my… Well… His binding was severed."

So it was as I'd suspected. The greater demon had taken advantage of the fact Elijah wouldn't give up his humanity while he had hope for a cure. Then through him, he had access to me and Camelot. It was a cunning plan, but that link was severed now. *Apparently*.

"I wouldn't lie to you about that," Elijah said, taking my silence to mean I didn't believe him. "Both sides of me care about you, Madeleine."

"Dark Elijah has a great way of showing it," I drawled.

He shrugged. "What can I say? I lack impulse control."

"Come back to Camelot with me."

"*No*."

"Ramona is an expert in soul medicine," I told him. "If anyone can help you find your way back, it's her." I didn't know why I left Issac out of the pitch. Ramona was the science and he was all about the spirit.

"Don't I get a consultation with the Light shrink?" Elijah drawled. "Does he make prison calls?"

I gasped. "How do you know about him?"

His eyes narrowed and he spoke slowly, "I can smell him on you."

"Can not."

"Can too."

"You're so full of it."

"You reek of *eau de good guy*."

"Elijah, *please*. I know your demon side is in

control, but I'm trying to help you. I still want to find your cure."

"Wake up, little lava girl. There is no cure for me, just a live autopsy and that's after the torture."

"You can't say that until we try everything." I shook my head. "Things have changed in Camelot. They accept me now."

"They accept you? Well, I guess you don't need me anymore. What happened to you walking in both worlds?"

I grabbed his wrist and dug my fingernails into his flesh. "Stop being such an arsehole."

"Have you kissed him yet?"

I sent a spark of power into him. "Don't ruin this, Elijah."

He lowered his gaze. "We should have left while we had the chance."

"You know I can't do that," I murmured. "I want to help you. I want you to be in my life, but not like this."

"I can't," he whispered. "It was bad enough last time."

"Bad?" I frowned, not understanding. "What do you mean? I know it wasn't a picnic, but—"

"It hurts," he interrupted. "I don't like going there."

It hurt for him to be in Camelot? My frustrations began to fade enough for my heart to hurt. He was hiding so much, but he didn't have to. Not with me. I knew if I kept pressing, he would lash out and his fancy container home would likely sink into a lava pit if I lost my cool—pun intended.

I slipped my palm from his wrist and took his hand. "If you won't let me help you, then can you help me?"

"You don't need my help," he replied, pulling away. "You managed just fine on that hill."

"He knows my true name, Elijah. The one attached to my Darkness."

This made him straighten up and take notice. "So he wasn't lying…"

I shook my head. "I may be able to do all those things, but if he comes back and uses it against me… I won't be able to stop him."

He thought for a moment, his eyes darkening. "The name is only a small part of you. Now you know it's there, you can isolate it. Easy. Problem solved."

"How?" I knew it wasn't going to be that simple. How could it? In our world, there was always another twist.

He shrugged like the answer was obvious. "Through the power of the mind."

"That's what Issac said."

Elijah scowled. "Maybe I should take you back to your stupid castle after all."

"Your demon side is such a dick," I snarked.

He laughed. "I have big dick energy."

"That's it. I'll find the portal on my own." I strode towards the door, but Elijah darted in front of me. "*Get out of my way.*"

"I'll take you," he promised. "It won't open until tomorrow. Just… Don't go. Not yet."

I hesitated, my power simmering with my annoyance.

"Madeleine, I don't want to be like this. I…" he trailed off and I swore he was on the verge of crying. "It's just… Some days the loss of my old life is harder to bear than others. The Darkness in me feeds off it and its… It's hard to stay afloat."

"Well," I said, hope blossoming in my heart, "that just means some of your Light still has control. It's like you said, we're all evolving."

"It doesn't feel like it."

"Elijah…" I threaded my fingers with his, attempting to draw out his humanity. It was time to ask the big questions, no matter the consequences. "Were you a Druid?"

"Yes," he replied. "I suppose I was something like that."

14

By the time the portal 'came around' again, another day had passed.

Elijah and I waited in the jungle, sitting side by side on a fallen tree. I was sure there was a snake camouflaged in a branch across from us, but he never mentioned it and I did my best to ignore the slithering creature. Needless to say, I didn't have any experience with literal jungles, just urban ones.

If it was one of his mysterious snake people, Elijah didn't let on. I was sure he wouldn't reveal the location of the portal if it was more than a regular reptile.

We'd slept in the same bed last night, but he'd remained tight-lipped on his admission of his Druidic heritage. I wasn't sure if it was because he couldn't remember or he didn't want to. Either way, that one sentence—*Yes. I suppose I was something like that*—was all I'd been given.

I picked up a stick and began to poke at the ground. "How do I know where the portal will lead?"

"Why?"

"I might want to come back."

He looked skeptical, but he replied, "You look into the surface."

"Is that it?"

"You're always looking for a more complicated answer." He snatched the stick out of my hand and threw it into the surrounding forest. "Things can be simple, you know."

I ignored his sour attitude. "I won't get flung into some alternate universe, will I?"

"The only portals I've encountered led to different parts of the Earth. Once, the Druids could open them to other universes, but not anymore. They were the only people who could."

He spoke about the Druids like he'd never been one of them. Recalling the image he'd accidentally shared with me the night he'd saved me from Ben Nevis, I felt an unbearable wave of melancholy. His life must have been peaceful until the Dark came—perhaps that's why he'd hidden himself in the rainforests of Borneo.

"Did you ever try to find the Darklands?" I asked.

"I'm a demon. I can't do those things," he replied cooly. "If you're just going to question me about things that don't matter anymore, you can forget about coming back."

"*Elijah*."

"You're still what you were," he hissed. "I lost *everything*."

I was either going to slap him or kill him, but instead, I kissed him. Seemed like the most appropriate gesture.

I fisted my hands into his shirt and pulled him against me, almost dragging him off the log. I was getting used to initiating this romance thing a little and it felt thrilling—more thrilling than calling forth all that lava.

A whooshing sound pulled us apart and we looked towards the noise to see the portal had opened. The air shimmered, radiating like a mirage on the horizon.

"There," Elijah said with a pout. "You can go back to your precious castle now."

I sighed. "You know this isn't goodbye."

"I'm not sure the kissing is enough to cancel out the nagging."

I smirked and shook my head. "Of course it is, you liar."

Elijah stilled and a smile tugged at his lips.

I stood and took a step towards the shimmering air. "Are you sure you don't want to come?"

"I'd rather go live with the snake people," he replied.

I was disappointed I wasn't enough for him to take a chance on finding a cure at Camelot, but it was his life. I couldn't force him.

I looked at him one last time, committing him and his silly rainforest to memory, then stepped through the portal.

The archive was dark when I stepped through the open door. I knew what to expect so my landing was smooth this time. Too bad there was no one around to witness the momentous occasion.

"I can't say I'm surprised you went through the portal," Aiden Thompson declared from somewhere in the gloom, "but you could have given us a heads-up."

I slapped my hand over my heart as if the motion would still its thundering beat. "Aiden."

He was sitting on a chair around the corner, watching me with tired eyes. His curly hair was unruly, and he was a little more rumpled than usual.

"I didn't see you there," I said sheepishly. I hoped my disappearance hadn't caused too much drama, but from the look on his face, I knew it was wishful thinking.

Aiden snorted. "I can see that."

I glanced at the portal. "How—"

"You left the door open," he said.

"I can explain. Greer—"

"It's your lucky day," he interrupted. "She wanted to see you the moment you got back."

"Aiden…"

"You seem to be a law onto yourself these days, Madeleine," he said, rising to his feet. "We're supposed to be a team."

"We are," I argued. "I didn't mean to go through

the portal. I—" I clamped my mouth shut, not knowing how much I should reveal about Elijah.

Aiden sighed and gestured for me to follow. "Come on, then. You can explain it to Greer."

We walked together to base camp in tense silence. Overhead, the sky was clear and a billion stars sparkled down on us. The icy air vaporised my breath and I huddled in my jacket, aware that my trousers and boots were still caked with mud from the rainforest.

"The portal works both ways," I told Aiden, explaining what Elijah had revealed. "We need to seal that door so nothing accidentally finds its way into the archive."

"Noted."

We stopped outside Greer's tent and Aiden swept open the flap. "Greer, Madeleine has returned."

The protector of the Codex and acting Inquisitor was sitting at a makeshift desk. Official-looking papers were stacked in front of her and a half-eaten meal had been pushed to one side. Greer was beautiful, lithe, and sweet, but she crackled with a formidable power I was becoming more and more aware of as my own power grew.

She nodded, her gaze moving to me. "Thank you, Aiden."

I waited until Aiden had left before I spoke. "Greer, I just want to—"

She held up her hand, silencing me. I waited as she closed a folder and straightened her desk, my gaze following her every move.

"It seems as if we're constantly rewriting the Codex these days," she mused after a moment. "Our past is a labyrinth of mystery, and our future is entirely unpredictable."

She didn't have to tell me twice.

"You remind me so much of Scarlett," she continued, her observation startling me. "Sometimes I wonder if a little of her rebelliousness joined with you the day she saved your soul. However, your mother tells me you've always been outside the box, so to speak."

I swallowed hard. "You spoke to my mother about me?"

"At great length." She studied me for a long moment, then added, "We are our own worst critics and our parents are our greatest champions… if we're lucky."

I nodded, not sure if this was a reprimand for disappearing again or a counselling session.

"What happened last night, Madeleine?"

"I stayed behind in the archive," I explained. "I was looking for something to help with my true name."

"And you went through the portal instead."

"It was Elijah," I blurted. "He took me through the portal."

"Elijah entered Camelot?" Her gaze met mine. "Why?"

"He loves me," I said, the worlds tumbling out of my mouth, "as best he can, and I…"

Greer sighed. "Love is a fickle thing, Madeleine. It

cannot be forced or tricked or manipulated. It is all too easily confused with lust."

"This isn't lust," I said, thinking about Issac. Was it possible to feel the same thing for two different men at the same time? Or was one lust? "I trust him. He's saved my life and helped me on more than one occasion."

"Are you certain of his motives?"

"He was trying to find a cure for his mutation when we first met. The Dark had been targeting me for a long time and he knew who I was…and what I'd been. He saved me once in London before he approached me about helping him."

"The incident at the nightclub?"

I nodded. "You know the rest, but…" I took a deep breath. "He was the one who slew Ikakantor the night Camelot was breeched, not me. He was bound to the greater demon and it was my fault the Dark could get into Camelot to begin with. The only way Elijah could sever his connection and save me was to submit to his Dark side. I wasn't powerful enough to stand against Ikakantor and Elijah sacrificed his…"

"His humanity?" Greer prompted.

"His, uh…" I lowered my gaze.

"You can trust me, Madeleine. Anything you say to me will not leave this tent."

"Elijah doesn't want to come here because he doesn't trust us," I told her. "If I betray his confidence, I might lose him forever and I can't… I…"

Greer leaned back and frowned, thinking over

what I'd told her. "All Elijah wants is a cure. Are you certain of this?"

"Yes."

Her Light flared and she sighed. Now that I was understanding my own abilities, I was picking up on more supernatural frequencies. There was a difference to Greer that I didn't feel in other Naturals. Perhaps it was the influence of the Codex, but she seemed to burn as brightly as Scarlett and Wilder. I wondered if she knew what I could see.

"If you can convince him to come, we will help him, but there are conditions."

"Of course," I blurted. The last thing I wanted was for her to change her mind.

"He must tell us what he knows of the Dark and cooperate fully with Ramona. He will be under constant guard until I say otherwise. His behaviour and his willingness to assist us will dictate our ongoing support."

"That's a lot of conditions."

"You're asking me to allow a demon inside the walls of Camelot," she said. "No matter what or who he was before, Darkness controls him now. I suspect his love for you is the only thing keeping it from completely ruling him. If it weren't the case, we'd already be breeched."

"I've already alerted Aiden about the portal."

Greer nodded. "And it will be dealt with."

"May I... May I return to Elijah tomorrow?"

"Only if Issac agrees to go with you. It is your

responsibility to convince him. I've extended as much as I and the Regula are willing to."

Talk about getting blood from a stone. Isaac was going to be mad at me anyway, but if I kept brining up Elijah, he was going to stonewall all my attempts.

"Understood," I muttered.

Greer narrowed her eyes and nodded. "Then you are dismissed."

I stood under the arch leading into the jousting field, watching Issac as he went through drills with his staff. His movements were slow and precise, his method as calm as the meditation he'd forced on me.

The muscles in his arm rippled as he flexed and I swallowed hard. He *was* handsome and it was only now that I realised I'd found it annoying because I wanted to hate him for the things he'd said when we'd first met. Now I kind of liked him and was about to mess it up again.

I took a deep breath and stepped onto the field.

"I spoke to Greer last night," he said without looking up. "I know about the portal and who came through it."

"What do you want me to say, Issac?" The gentle persuasion tactics I'd been mulling over all night had just gone out the window.

"I'm concerned your judgement is impaired," he stated. "Elijah is a demon, Madeleine."

"Not all of him," I argued. "And it's the part of him that's not I'm trying to save."

"That part of him is gone. You admitted it yourself."

"Arsehole!" I threw my hands into the air. "You're twisting my words. Greer permitted it."

"Only if I agree to go through the portal with you." He set down his staff. "And I'm not agreeing."

"You're forgetting who I am."

"I haven't forgotten at all."

"Then why won't you let me help him?"

Issac turned his back on me and picked up his hoodie. He dragged it over his head, messing up his hair.

"You're jealous."

He scoffed and glared at me over his shoulder. "I confided in you, Madeleine."

"And I never told a soul."

Issac turned. "You have feelings for him, don't you?"

On the verge of tears, I sank down onto the bleachers and let my head fall into my hands. "I've tried. I'm *trying*. I've gone from being the most hated person in Camelot to the most revered, and I don't know what you want me to do. I don't know how to *be* or what to *feel*. I don't know what love is or who I should feel it for."

"Madeleine…"

"You seem to know what to do with so much certainty, it clouds you to everything else. Do you want me for yourself? I don't know if *I* want *me*. Then Elijah, he—"

"*Madeleine*." Issac placed his hands on my shoulders and my gaze snapped up to meet his. "Calm yourself."

A tremor rumbled the field and I sniffed. "Did I…?"

"Yes." He sighed and looked around the structure as the earth settled. "Well, at least I know you meant what you said. What are we going to do?"

I got the feeling the last question was rhetorical and I remained silent. Instead, I breathed in through my nose and out through my mouth.

"Elijah knows things," I told him, thankful he wasn't pressing any more of my buttons—especially the one labelled 'romance', "about the Dark, about what I could be, about Ikakantor. He knows about portals and true names."

"How convenient," Issac drawled.

"I think… I-I think he's been alive for a long time," I murmured. "A *very* long time."

"He's not a greater demon in disguise, is he?"

"No."

"But you know why."

Issac was on to me, but I wasn't going to betray Elijah, just as I hadn't betrayed Issac. "There are things he's told me in confidence. If he wants to tell you, then that's his choice."

He sighed. "Those things aren't enough."

"Those 'things' are everything," I said. "If the

tables were turned, wouldn't you want me to honour your wishes?"

"Madeleine, we're talking about letting a demon into Camelot."

"So you keep saying." I threw my hands into the air. "After everything I've been through to get here, you keep insulting me. I'm part demon, too." It was one thing alluding to it but saying it out loud was oddly freeing. *I was part demon.*

Issac stilled, though his expression was still cloudy.

"Elijah could be an informant for our cause regardless of our existing relationship," I said, laying it all on the line. "If Ramona can learn about his mutation and help him, she might gain more insight about my situation. This isn't about personal feelings."

"It is though, isn't it?"

I cursed under my breath. "I'd have more luck beating my head against a brick wall than talking to you."

"Now who's insulting who?"

"Insults born out of frustration," I fired back.

Issac turned his gaze onto the sky, his thoughts unknown. I withdrew into myself, doing my best to contain my power. I still hadn't worked out how to separate my emotions from them, and I wasn't sure I could. Maybe it was something that'd come with age but until then, I'd just be a hot-headed twenty-something.

"I'll go with you," Issac said. "But I'm calling the shots."

I looked up at him. "Really?"

"You have some valid points," he said, his voice low. "But I will watch him like a hawk. The moment he puts a foot wrong, he'll answer to me."

My heart leapt. "Don't make any judgements until you meet him. Despite our differences, we all want the same things."

Issac shook his head. "Inviting the enemy into Camelot. *Shite*." It was the first time I'd heard him swear and I raised my eyebrows. Curse words kind of suited him. "When are we going on this foolish mission?"

"Tonight."

"Tonight?" He sighed and picked up his staff. "Nothing is ever simple with you, is it, Madeleine Greenbriar?"

"Nope," I replied with a grimace. "And it's not likely to change anytime soon.

15

—————

The archive was quiet as Issac and I waited for the portal to swing around to the rainforest.

I watched the black surface ripple as a cool breeze from outside wound its way into the foyer.

"Do you think all of these doors have portals behind them?" I wondered out loud.

"Maybe," Issac replied. "I don't think we should open them, just in case."

"It might be more exciting. So far, all we've uncovered Camelot's HM Revenue & Customs. Did you know people paid for things with silver pennies and farthings? And if they didn't have enough small coins, they cut them into quarters? What a nightmare."

Issac chuckled softly. "That's what you're thinking about?"

I shrugged. "What else should I be thinking about?"

"Maybe what you will say to the demon when we find him."

I scowled. "I figure it will come to me in the moment."

"Here," he said, handing me a sword hilt. "I got something for you."

"My arondight blade?" I turned the metal over in my hands, surprised he'd even found it. I was sure Thompson still had it under lock and key just to spite me.

"You might need it."

"I don't really need a sword anymore," I told him, "but thank you."

"It's a tool, not a crutch," he said. "Tools can be useful."

His view on the matter was the complete opposite of Elijah's and for a moment, it was startling. They were oil and water, which was a bleak omen for the meeting to come.

"Elijah can be skittish and will lash out if he feels threatened," I explained. "He can be… Well, he can be a bit of an arsehole."

"And you told me not to make judgements until I met him."

"It's his Dark side," I said with a sigh. "When it wasn't in control, he was the complete opposite."

"Well, if Ramona can crack his mutation, then we'll find out." He checked his watch. "How do you know where the portal is pointing?"

"Elijah said to look into the surface and we'll know."

Issac scowled and raised his eyebrows. "Seriously?"

"He said, 'You're always looking for a more complicated answer. Things can be simple, you know.' Or something like that."

"This guy sounds like a bag of fun," he drawled.

Choosing not to bite, I stared into the portal, wondering how I was supposed to see the destination when it was black as night.

The longer I stared, the more cross-eyed I became, but eventually, I fancied I saw some images ripple through the surface of the portal. Was that a tree? Perhaps it was a vine, or that lump was a rock.

I squinted, attempting to focus the blurry objects into some clarity. Just when I thought my eyeballs were about to explode, I realised I was looking at the rainforest.

Elijah was right. It was nothing more than an optical illusion. I could see the way through now that my brain had wrapped its way around the concept.

"It's open," I said. "It's an illusion."

"You were right," Issac replied, squinting at the rippling surface. "I can see a forest beyond. It's blurry and dark, but there's definitely something there."

"C'mon." I stepped through the door, hoping I'd have a smooth landing…and in the right place.

The air was hot and sticky as I emerged from the portal.

Dense rainforest wrapped around the little clearing like a thick blanket, obscuring the entire world. I breathed in the scents of damp earth and rain and looked towards the sky. It was daylight in this part of the world, and the sun sent dappled rays through the dense canopy.

Issac appeared beside me, looking around with a surprised expression. "I knew you said he was in a rainforest but… Where in the world are we?"

"Borneo." I gestured at him to keep it down. "There are more things here that want to eat us besides demons."

"Like?"

"Tigers, panthers, sun bears…snake people."

"Snake people?" Issac hissed as exotic bird calls echoed in the distance. "Seriously?"

I cast out my senses, using my power as a glorified radar. Remembering the general direction to Elijah's house, I led the way, keeping my eyes peeled for trouble. Not that I thought we'd run into any Balan demons out here, but I wasn't kidding about the big cats or the snakes. I got Maisy to Google it for me before we left.

"I didn't realise it'd be so humid," Issac murmured as we forced our way through the dense growth.

"We're close to the equator here," I replied. "The heat and rain makes the air heavy."

"If I ever want to go somewhere tropical for a holiday, remind me I'm not a fan of humidity."

I smirked and pushed past a large palm leaf. As it

snapped back, and almost hit Issac in the face, I stilled. My power swept over an anomaly, flaring through my body with a warning.

"He's here." I stopped and looked around the jungle, but it was too thick to see far. "I can feel him."

Issac opened his mouth to reply, but Elijah landed in front of him and shoved him with the flats of both hands. He must've been hanging in the treetops, watching us.

"You brought the pretty boy priest?" he exclaimed. "*I can't believe you.*"

"I'm not a priest," Issac said, recovering quickly.

"You're a spiritual shrink. That makes you a priest."

"*Stop it,*" I exclaimed.

"When you said you might come back, I didn't think it would be with that guy," he said to me. "I only invited you, Madeleine."

"I'm here to make sure you don't harm her," Issac declared.

"Madeleine doesn't need protection. She can handle herself."

"She shouldn't have to handle everything on her own," he fired back.

"I'm not into threesomes," Elijah drawled. "At least not with guys like you."

"Elijah, just calm down so we can talk," I urged. "We've come to—"

"What's he got that I don't?" he demanded, interrupting me. "I've got a nice house *and* a car—a big four-wheel drive, perfect for jungle exploration.

And I've got magical powers, but mine are way more fun than his."

"A house you stole," I replied, ignoring the rest.

"That guy didn't need it. He could've spent the money on sick orphans in a third world country, but he spent it on himself. Do you know how far two million American dollars can go?"

"This guy is a bag of contractions," Issac said to me. "A demon caring about human orphans? Really?"

"Shut your face, pretty boy, before I shut it for you," Elijah shouted. "I thought priests were supposed to be celibate, yet here you are trying to steal my girl and rubbing my face in it."

"She's your girl?" Issac snorted. "That's up to Madeleine. Though I can't see why she'd want you."

"I don't see why she'd want you, either," Elijah exclaimed. "You're as exciting as a pile of panther shite. Your face looks like you've been sucking on a lemon a monkey shat out of its arsehole."

"Maybe she wants me because I'm a man and you're little more than a child."

Elijah let out a strangled cry and launched himself at Issac. The pair collided and began to throw punches.

To be honest, they both put up a pretty good fight. Elijah gave Issac a bloodied nose and Issac sunk an impressive right hook into Elijah's eye.

Darkness wrapped around Light as they wrestled and I sighed. I knew this was going to be a difficult operation, but this was next level. As they began to choke one another with their power, I stamped my foot before someone got really hurt.

"Stop it!" I shouted, the ground cracking. A fissure splintered between the two men and broke them apart. It was a tiny fracture in the forest floor, but it was more than enough to slap some sense into them.

"Holy shite," Elijah murmured. His right eye socket was puffed up, so he squinted at the ground out of his left.

Issac wiped at his bloodied nose and glared at him. "This was a waste of time."

"I'll say," Elijah bit back. "If you wanted to break up with me, Madeleine, you didn't have to bring your new boy toy here to make a point."

"He's not—" I pursed my lips and breathed in through my nose. "Neither of you are. Not right now."

"Then it was nice knowing you." He turned, intending to disappear into the rainforest, but I grabbed his arm.

"I've come to convince you to return to Camelot with me."

Elijah pulled away and glared at Issac. "I already told you no."

"And I told you, I'm not giving up on your cure."

He snorted, his glare intensifying. "And are you going to take me by force? Is that why he's here?"

"He's here because the Regula ordered it," I told him. "You've got clearance, Elijah. You're permitted to come back with us. They're going to help you."

"*But...*"

"There are conditions," Issac said. "And they must be adhered to at all times, otherwise—"

Elijah grunted and jabbed a finger at him. "Otherwise it's that live autopsy your kind would love to subject me to. Don't think I know you won't spend the entire time baiting me, just hoping I'll put a foot wrong."

"You don't even know me," Issac stated.

"I know enough."

I put my hand on Elijah's arm, my touch settling his rising anger. My power simmered and reached for him, the threads of silver and red Light wanting to jump into his mind. I held it steady, not wanting to spook him or accidentally influence his decisions.

"If we can cure you, then you might get your power back," I argued. "Isn't it worth the chance?"

"What power?" he scoffed. "Anything I had was lost a long time ago."

"Your Colours," I replied. "Your… prism."

Elijah froze.

"He's a Druid?" Issac exclaimed. "Why am I only finding this out now?"

"*Suspected* Druid," Elijah stated.

"What do you mean *suspected*?" I demanded. "You told me!"

He shrugged. "I forget a lot of things."

"You haven't forgotten," I hissed. "You're just afraid to face it."

"I believe I said, 'I suppose I was something like that'," Elijah snapped. "It isn't my fault you took it literally."

"Demons lie, Madeleine," Issac stated. "He's not a Druid. He's just a desperate human."

"No, I saw it," I argued. "I know who he used to be. I know who he still is. That guy is worth finding a cure for."

Elijah sighed, "I told you once before. If I'm cured, I could wither and die. I like life too much."

I shook my head. "You like living on your own in a remote rainforest and making friends with snake people?"

"Beats dealing with prejudiced jerks like Issac." He snorted. "I mean, what kind of name is that anyway?"

I grabbed his arm, pulling his focus away from Issac. "It's not guaranteed," I murmured. "But we have a real chance, Elijah."

He shook his head. "I can't. I told you. Camelot… It hurts to be there."

"Hurts, how?"

He glanced at Issac and I noticed his right eye was opening up again.

"Forget about him," I said. "Focus on me." His gaze moved to mine. "Are you talking about memories? Of Camelot?"

"No. I won't go. It's been too long."

I wasn't giving up. "What if we could isolate your Darkness so you could come back?"

"*No.*"

Issac glared at Elijah and took my arm. "C'mon, Madeleine. He isn't worth it."

"No," I snapped, wrenching away.

Elijah snorted. "He's right. I'm having too much fun as a demon."

"You wouldn't be hiding yourself away in this rainforest if that was true," I argued. "You're trying to protect people."

"Is that what you call it?"

"I'd call it hiding like a coward," Issac stated. "He's not going to change his mind. He's too selfish."

"Selfish?" Elijah exclaimed, his Darkness flaring. "I gave up everything to save Madeleine and your stupid castle." He fisted his hands into the front of Issac's shirt and wrenched him close. "I came here to protect her from the Dark. I couldn't care less about you."

"Then why do you treat her like that? Huh?"

Elijah's expression twisted and he shoved Issac with his Darkness, forcing the Natural to fall on his arse across the clearing.

"Don't ruin this," I whispered, tugging on his sleeve as Issac growled in anger.

"Why do you keep trying to save me?" he wailed. "I just want to be left alone."

"That's a lie. That's just the mutation talking. It isn't you. I've seen who you are, Elijah, and it's not this childish arsehole. You're kind, thoughtful, wise, brave… strong. You can be those things again, but you have to come with me."

He took a step back, the confusion clear in his features. He was going through an internal struggle neither Issac nor I understood.

"If I leave, it's forever," I said. "Do you really want that?"

Elijah's expression fell. "*Madeleine.*"

"I've made my offer. Now it's up to you to choose." I held out my hand. "Do you want to fight? Or do you want to hide?"

His gaze bored into mine and I almost believed I could see all the Colours he'd lost. The prism of Light the Druids used to create their magic—complex shapes and structures more intricate than any geometric pattern on Earth. The anguish of losing that had been eating away at him for centuries and this was all that was left of him.

How could he have hope when he'd had none before? Well, not until he'd met me in that stupid nightclub in London.

Finally, Elijah slipped his hand into mine.

"I want to go home," he whispered. "*Please.*"

16

It was a long wait for the portal to return to Camelot.

We stayed the night in Elijah's fancy shipping container house, and Issac kept as far away from him as he could. I was a buffer between the pair and keeping my cool was more trying than battling Ikakantor's visions.

Explaining the terms of his stay at Camelot wasn't pleasant, but even he realised there had to be a little give on his behalf if he wanted to find a cure…and keep me in his life.

When all three of us finally made it back to the clearing, we wasted no time stepping through the shimmering air and returning to Camelot.

Greer and Ramona were waiting for us in the archive when we arrived. They were flanked by two Natural guards, both armed and ready to strike if the need arose.

"So this is the infamous Elijah," Greer said,

looking him over as the two guards sealed the portal behind us.

"Who's this fancy lady?" he drawled, already embarrassing me.

"This is Greer," I told him. "She's the protector of the Codex *and* the Inquisitor."

"Oh, so she's *the boss*."

Greer pursed her lips, but I wasn't sure if she was trying to hold in laughter or displeasure.

He peered at Ramona and grinned. "Ah, the woman who left me with three gnarly scars on my chest. Do you want to see?"

He went to lift up his shirt and I placed a hand on his wrist.

"I can see my immediate future will not be boring," Ramona said, giving me a look that said everything.

"I know right?" Elijah added. "I was comatose last time."

"Gentlemen," Greer declared, "if you wouldn't mind escorting our guest down to the infirmary, Madeleine and I will be along shortly."

The guards ushered Elijah towards the stairs. Ramona followed, shooting a reassuring glance over her shoulder.

Greer nodded towards the group climbing the stairs. "Issac, if you wouldn't mind accompanying them?"

He glowered but nodded. "As you wish."

"As you wish!" Elijah exclaimed with a laugh. "Pompous twat!"

I closed my eyes with a groan. If I was going for first impressions, this wasn't playing out as well as I'd hoped.

"Sorry," I muttered.

"His demonic tendencies are…" I knew Greer was thinking of a polite way to put it, but she didn't have to.

"Childish?" I offered.

"Yes, something like that."

"He wasn't like this until he severed the link to his humanity," I told her. "He—"

"Oh, I believe you Madeleine. We've seen much worse behaviour."

"What's going to happen to him?"

"I've discussed this with Ramona at length," Greer replied. "She will do whatever she can to work this out, you have our word on that. Then it's up to Elijah to hold up his end of the deal."

"He wasn't happy about it," I admitted. "I just hope he doesn't act out. He seems… Well, stranger than usual."

"If Ramona can isolate his mutation, as she did yours, this behaviour will be a thing of the past."

I stared after them, but the archive was empty. "I hope so."

"Now that we have a moment, I wanted to see how you were coping with all of this." She looked around the archive as if she was lost in thought. "It must be a lot for you, Madeleine."

I raised my eyebrows. "You wanted to check on me?"

"Is it so strange?" She laughed, and I understood why Scarlett had always been dark about her. Greer was perfect.

"You're the leader of the Naturals and I'm…" I trailed off with a shrug.

"You're growing into a strong young woman. I'm not sure there's a name for your new abilities, but your heart remains as good as the day I first met you at the London Sanctum."

"When I was almost taken over by Human Convergence, you mean?" I snorted and gave my head a shake. "Not my finest moment."

"Perhaps not, but you've overcome it and much more."

"Wilder and Scarlett had a lot to do with that," I murmured. "And Ramona, Jackson, and Esme. A lot of people, actually."

"You shouldn't underestimate your own part in your story," Greer said. "And Elijah's. He will look to you before his own ordeal is over."

"I know."

We stood in silence for a moment, soaking in the strange atmosphere of the archive. I could sense the sickly power leaking from the vault through multiple layers of dense limestone, but I couldn't recall if I'd felt it all the way up here before.

"How is Wilder and Scarlett?" I asked, hopeful I might get some kind of answer, no matter how vague. "Has there been any change?" It had been a month since they'd fallen into a coma, and there had been no word. I was getting jealous of everyone who had top secret clearance.

Greer pursed her lips, which wasn't good. "Speaking of that, I have to check on Masters." She glanced towards the stairs with a frown.

I sighed, not surprised by her evasion at all. I had to resist the temptation to reach out and do a deep dive into her brain. Not only would it be a personal violation, I'd be chained up in a cell below Glastonbury before I could say boo.

"Is he still down there?" I asked. If that was the case, Masters was becoming a little more obsessed than I first thought.

"He insists he's made progress, but I'll be the judge of that."

"Am I permitted to see Elijah? I loathe to think what will happen to him if I leave him alone with Ramona."

"Ramona can look after herself," Greer said with a fleeting smile. "Did you know we've known each other since our academy days?"

I shook my head. "I didn't realise you were in the same class."

"We were for a time. Fiercely competitive is her middle name. I think that's why she makes such a good physician." She had a faraway look in her eyes as she recalled her youth. "No, Ramona can look after herself." Greer turned to me and gestured towards the stairs. "Go on. She might need an assistant."

"Thank you."

I moved off as she ventured the other way, not

sure what I should be more worried about—Issac and Elijah punching each other again, Ikakantor returning with more demons, the vault opening despite Masters' best efforts, Wilder and Scarlett being trapped in a coma forever, or me accidentally turning the planet into an ocean of lava.

I paused on the bottom step and looked over my shoulder as Greer disappeared downstairs.

Where did we go from here? Just like usual, I didn't have any answers.

Issac was waiting outside the infirmary when I arrived.

I lingered outside the door of the prefabricated building, waiting to hear what gem of advice he was going to impart on me before I went inside. At least we didn't have to hang out in a tent with thin canvas walls.

"Despite his lack of respect, foul mouth, and unpredictable violent outbursts, that man seems to think he loves you," he declared.

"You say it like it's an impossibility," I drawled.

"That a demon can love? Of course it is."

I narrowed my eyes. "That's not what I was referring to."

Issac sighed and lowered his gaze. "That's not what I meant. I'm sorry, it just came out the wrong way."

"Careful, Issac, your prejudice is showing again."

"I already apologised," he said. "What more do I need to say?"

"It's not about what you said."

"Isn't it?" he asked. "Back in the rainforest I... implied some things in the heat of the moment."

I hesitated before I said, "That you didn't mean."

"Oh, I meant them."

All at once, I felt a wave of uncomfortable embarrassment heat my cheeks. My inexperience was showing again, and I didn't like it.

He was saying he wanted more with me without actually saying the words. No wonder being embroiled in a romance was as confusing as it was exciting. No one wanted to admit to anything for fear of being emotionally vulnerable. Naturals were the worst at showing their true selves. During times of war, weaknesses could be exploited and we were trained to hide them, which meant it didn't lend well to moments like this.

"I'm just as surprised as you are," Issac murmured.

"It's... I just..." I took a deep breath. "I'm not in a good place right now." I glanced at the infirmary door. "I'm stuck between a lot of things. Evolution and...well, I don't know."

"Are you really sure he's the right man for you?"

I wasn't sure Issac and I were on the right page. Did he want me for *who* I was? Or were his feelings despite *what* I was? It was a fine line and only one was true and right.

Greer had it the proper way around when she said love couldn't be forced.

Still, I wasn't sure what I felt for who. Elijah was dangerous and exciting, while Issac was safe and trustworthy.

"I don't know, but despite everything that's happened to him, Elijah trusts me," I replied. "He needs someone to fight for him. Right now, that's all that matters."

"I hope you know what you're doing."

"Save it, Issac." I snorted and pushed past him.

Ramona wasn't in the infirmary when I entered, but two guards were. Elijah was sitting in a chair beside a stainless-steel table full of medical equipment with his sleeve rolled up. When he saw me, he smiled.

"Do you like my new friends?" he asked, grinning at the two Naturals who'd been assigned to his guard detail. "I call them Bob one and Bob two."

I looked at the two men and asked, "Are either of you named Bob?"

"Nope," the guy on the left replied, looking unimpressed. He was a typical Natural—tall, muscled, and uptight. "I'm Smith and he's Thatcher."

Elijah laughed. "Still *bland*."

"English," I told him with a sigh. "They're English, not bland." They looked similar, to be honest.

"Worst assignment ever," Smith muttered.

"Can you give us a moment?" I nodded towards the door.

"We have our orders," Thatcher replied, tightening his grip on his arondight blade.

I raised my eyebrows. "What harm can he do with me here?"

"'No offence, miss, but you helped him escape before."

"I also gave Camelot a moat full of lava and saved your arse," I fired back.

"I love it when you get all snappy like that," Elijah quipped. "It's sexy as hell."

Smith rolled his eyes and nudged Thatcher. "We'll be just outside, but no funny business."

Elijah snorted as the two men left us alone, sniggering to himself. "*No funny business.* Is he serious?"

"You're not helping yourself," I scolded. "Everyone thinks you're a fool."

"This place is like a field day for the Darkness inside me," he complained. "Everyone rises to the occasion."

"Well, hopefully you can learn to control yourself."

"Don't sound so disappointed. You wanted me to come here."

"I am a little," I admitted. "I want… I want this to work for you. I want you to get your life back."

The stupid smile faded from his face and he held out his hand. I took it without thinking and our powers brushed together—his Darkness and my… I had to figure out what to call it.

"You need to watch that vault of yours," he said in a moment of clarity. "It's trying to get out."

"What do you mean?" I asked, my brow furrowing. "Have you been in the archive before you came to get me?"

"No. Just that once," he replied with a shrug. "I'm not a complete idiot."

"Good. I wouldn't know how to explain it to the Regula."

"That guy down there…"

"Who?" I paused. "Masters?"

He nodded and tapped his temple. "Watch him, okay?"

"We've got this handled, Elijah. Don't worry about it."

"No one believed me, but you need to listen. It wants to get out and it *will*."

His words were troubling, but ever since he'd stepped through the portal his demon side seemed to have gone haywire.

"You can't keep going around saying strange things and not explain yourself," I urged. "You're here to get help, not remind everyone how offensive demons can be."

"Screw Light and Dark," he hissed. "I fight for *you*. You asked me. You asked me and that's what I said."

His hand slipped from mine and he blinked as Ramona appeared out of the room at the back, her trusty tablet in her hands.

"Oh, Madeleine, there you are," she said. "Do you like our new infirmary? It's less draughty."

"It's great." I flashed Elijah a warning glare. "He isn't giving you any trouble, is he?"

"So far so good," she told me. "Though his running commentary is worthy of an A-list comedy routine."

"See, *she* likes me," he grumbled.

Ramona smiled and looked around the infirmary. "Where did the Bobs go?"

"Not you, too," I groaned and Elijah chuckled.

"Do you want my shirt off yet, doc?" he asked, wiggling his eyebrows up and down. "Madeleine's here, so it's the perfect time to get my kit off."

"You're a real charmer," she said laughing. "Take it off then. I want to stick some electrodes on your chest to get some readings while you sleep."

"Ooh. *Electrodes*." He grinned wickedly at me, his earlier outburst forgotten.

"When you're poking around in there, can you find his arsehole switch and turn it off, too?" I asked.

"Sure thing." Ramona smirked and glanced at Elijah. "I was planning on it."

17

The archive was already full of Naturals working on manuscripts when I ventured into the city the following day.

Since Elijah had returned with us, Issac had loosened our training timetable so he could keep his fingers is everyone's pies. It sounded dirtier than it actually was, but his distrust of all things demonic was making him a little twitchy-eyed. So, I checked on Masters and the vault.

After Elijah's crazy ramblings about my old Light Studies teacher, I thought it was best to double-check the poor guy hadn't starved himself to death or gone crazy trying to create his barrier.

My stomach began to gurgle and groan as I approached the professor and the massive vault door. After a month working on the barrier, Masters had created something spectacular, but I knew it still wasn't enough.

"Madeleine," he said, looking up from his work. "Hello."

"How are you going with the barrier?" I asked with a smile.

"So-so. Can you still feel the leak?"

"A little, but it's much better," I replied, not wanting to let him down. I was afraid he might snap if I told him it was just the same, then fall off his perch if I mentioned I could feel it up in the foyer. I made a mental note to raise it with Greer when I went back to base camp.

"You know, Greer gave me the same look last night as you're giving me right now."

"I'm worried about you," I admitted. "You're down here for twenty-three hours out of the day. A lack of vitamin D can have adverse effects, you know."

"Oh, don't worry about me," he said with a wave of his hand. "This is the ultimate puzzle and solving it will take the ultimate sacrifice."

"I hope you don't mean you'll die trying."

Masters laughed, the sound echoing down the hall. "Of course not!"

Footsteps behind me drew my gaze and I turned to see Trent walking towards us.

"Madeleine, there you are," he said. "I've been looking for you everywhere."

"What's up?" I asked, leaving Masters to his work.

"Greer has summoned you."

"She has? Good, because I need to speak to her."

"Two birds, one stone," he replied. "Ramona has some results."

My heart leapt, excited there was something to report so soon. I hoped it was good news because we all needed a little sunshine right about now.

We walked down to base camp together in the drizzling rain, the vault forgotten for the moment. Water beaded on our black waterproof jackets like little diamonds and sparkled as we moved. Looking at the sky, I wondered when we'd get the first snow of the season. It was chilly enough to turn at any moment.

Trent coughed nervously and asked, "So you and the hybrid, huh?"

I let out a *humph*. "How long have you been working up the courage to ask me that?"

"I should've asked you when you brought him into Camelot the first time."

"Well, you let us go."

"That was after you attacked me in that human village." Trent laughed as we sidestepped a group of researchers and scientists venturing up to the archive. They gave us curious glances as we passed, but no one spoke. "Who would've thought we'd end up here?"

"Not me," I admitted, wondering what Ramona had found out about Elijah's condition.

"Do you think Ikakantor will attack again?"

"Yes," I replied. "But I don't think it will be so direct next time."

Trent grunted as we arrived at camp. "He's running out of demons to do his bidding."

"We never knew how many were here to begin with, so who knows."

"Maybe your boyfriend does."

I pursed my lips and shrugged. "Maybe…"

When we arrived, Greer was already lingering outside the infirmary. She wore a black woollen coat with a beige scarf wrapped around her neck, and her almond-coloured hair was loose and waving in the breeze. My long, straight, black hair looked lifeless and stringy compared to hers.

I picked up on Trent's nerves as we stopped before her and smirked. He had a crush on the acting Inquisitor, but which man didn't?

"Thank you, Trent," she said. "You may return to your duties."

He bowed his head and scurried off, leaving us alone.

"I was just speaking to Masters in the archive," I began.

"I see."

"The barrier isn't working," I told her. "Nothing has changed, and I'm worried it's getting worse. I sensed echoes upstairs when we returned last night."

"I suspected as much." She looked troubled but urged me towards the infirmary. "Come. Ramona has some results she wants to discuss."

"Is that it?"

"For the time being."

We entered the infirmary and I became uneasy when I saw it was empty save for Ramona and Issac.

I swallowed hard. "Where's Elijah?"

"We have moved him to a more secure location," Greer explained. "Thompson is overseeing the facility."

"Thompson?" I groaned.

"It's merely for the time being," she added. "No one will harm him as long as he doesn't harm others."

Issac snorted, earning himself a trademark Madeleine Greenbriar withering glare.

"What have you found out?" I asked with a hopeful spark in my heart.

"A great deal for such a short amount of time. As you know, his previous test results were inconclusive," Ramona began. "Elijah wasn't human before they mutated him—at least, he was nothing like modern humans, though Issac told me of your suspicions."

"I'm positive he was once a Druid, though he keeps trying to convince us otherwise," I said. "He admitted it a few days ago, then denied it the next. He's skirted around his past more times than I care to count."

"It's a likely explanation, but we have nothing to compare it to," Ramona said. "It's not like we understand Druid physiology. This may be the closest thing we've ever had to a blood sample. I'm completely in the dark."

"What about his mutation?"

"It's nothing like Human Convergence," Issac said. "He's infected with something else. He was never the same as you, Madeleine."

Ignoring Issac, I looked at Ramona. He was just

looking for a way to exile Elijah for good, but I wasn't going to let him.

"Explain it to me," I demanded.

"It's Elijah, but it isn't…" she began. "He has two halves, which means he's coexisting with a demon who has developed as a mirror image of his true self. They've become so twisted, there isn't a way to tell them apart."

"A two-headed snake," Issac said, curling his lip.

"Get over it," I snapped.

"He's aware of what he's doing, but he doesn't have control," he told me with a scowl. "Which is dangerous considering he has Darkness at his disposal."

"That he never used against you, by the way," I reminded him. "He bloodied your nose all on his own."

"I'm fairly certain I don't want an explanation," Greer stated before turning to Ramona. "Is there any way to separate the two halves?"

"It's almost like he's afraid to come forth," she explained. "Like he's hiding behind his demon."

"When we went to the rainforest to get him, he said he didn't like being at Camelot because it hurt," I told her. "It was as if he was shrinking away from something that'd happened to him before they took him."

"I don't blame him," Ramona went on. "If he's as old as we think he is, the things he must have been through…" She lowered her gaze and studied her tablet. "Which brings me to my next observation."

I sighed. "There's more?" As if Elijah being all twisted up with a malignant demonic growth wasn't enough, there was a punchline, too.

"Your blood shows similarities to his," Ramona said, cutting to the chase like a punch in the gut. "Startling similarities."

I frowned, but what she was saying wasn't out of the realm of possibilities. We were both mutated with demon DNA.

"Similarities? How?" I asked.

"I know you're thinking I mean your demonic mutations, and you'd be right, but it's more than that." She flipped around her tablet so I could see the grainy black and white image. It looked like a terrible photocopy with several lines of black smudges.

"What is this exactly?"

"This is your DNA, Madeleine. Those marks are your genes." She swiped her finger across the screen, revealing another image similar to the first. "And this is Elijah's."

I shook my head, not understanding what all the little lines meant. "What does it mean?"

"Whatever Elijah was before he was mutated, matches the unknown parts of your current development."

"I knew it," Issac said. "The way you called on that fire…"

"Hang on," I said holding up my hands. "Let's not get ahead of ourselves here."

"The science stands up," Ramona said as she

glanced at Greer. "Madeleine appears to be part Druid. Whatever was used in her strain of Human Convergence must have included DNA from multiple sources."

"Then why didn't it manifest in the other victims?" Greer asked.

Ramona shrugged. "It's merely speculation, but I believe it's all linked back to Scarlett."

"Arondight triggered something the day she saved Madeleine's soul," Greer murmured. "More than just linking the mutation."

I didn't like how they were talking about me like I wasn't in the same room.

"I can barely understand one life, but three?" I exclaimed.

"You *are* a triune, Madeleine," Ramona said. "A little of all three known supernatural species."

"Yeah? I guess you haven't heard about the snake people then," I drawled.

"Snake people?" Greer glanced at Issac, who shrugged.

"I'm not a Druid," I went on, my mind attempting to wrap around this absurd information. "I don't have Colours or prisms or whatever they have to make their spells. My Light and Darkness have melted into one, that's all."

"DNA doesn't lie," Ramona breathed. "What that means for your abilities… Well, we're still in unknown territory."

I looked at Greer and began to understand her interest in me. Ever since she'd seen me rip apart the hillside outside Camelot, she'd been real nice and accommodating.

It was clear now—the Regula wanted to use me as a weapon against the Dark.

I scowled, knowing the responsibility of stepping into the shoes of the Twin Flames was more than I could handle. I had a demonic true name, and now I could have a Druidic one, too. I could nullify Light, kill demons with my bare hands, walk inside people's minds and change their memories, call upon the fire of the Earth, and who knows what else. Next I'd be shapeshifting into a hawk like the druidess Gilhana had in Scarlett's stories.

"I don't care about me," I snapped, shoving the unwelcome revelations aside. "What about Elijah? Can you help him or not?"

Ramona set down the tablet and turned off the screen. "It's complicated…"

"Complicated how?"

"It's a psychological issue," Issac said. "Until he wants to return to what he once was, he will stay the same."

"You're saying that all this time he had the power to…" I shook my head.

"Not exactly," Ramona explained. "He will have to fight the demon, but I have to remove it at the root —his soul. It has to be a combined effort, or it won't work."

My hopes began to rise. "But he can be cured?"

"We won't know for sure until we try."

"And he isn't exactly a willing patient," Issac

quipped. Elijah must have been making things difficult, which was likely the real reason he wasn't here to discuss his treatment.

"Then I'll talk to him," I said. "Right now."

"*Madeleine.*"

I strode across the infirmary and shoved open the door, ignoring Issac's calls. There was no way in hell I was going to sit back and let Elijah sabotage his cure. Not after all the trouble he went through to get me to help him.

After eight hundred years living with a demonic infestation, he deserved his life back.

After picking up on Elijah in the rainforest, I now had a good idea how to sense his presence amongst the Naturals. I focused on the immediate camp area and found him in a Light-enclosed tent near the main training yard.

When I pushed my way past the guard stationed outside, Thompson gave me a frosty reception and was less than impressed when I demanded to take Elijah into Camelot.

"You get one whiff of power and now you think you're above the law?" he asked with a scowl.

"Don't talk to the lady like that," Elijah snapped. He was sitting on a chair in the middle of the tent, looking sour.

"No one asked you," Thompson spat.

"We'll bring his guards," I told him.

He glared at me. "It seems like I have no choice."

That's how Elijah and I found ourselves in the ruins of Camelot, followed at a distance by the Bobs. It was our version of a long walk on a beach at sunset.

"They didn't mistreat you, did they?" I asked as we walked through the lower city.

"They could have given me a magazine," he grumbled.

I chuckled and shook my head. "That's what you're worried about?"

"I only worry about immediate discomforts."

Stopping before a broken statue, I sensed the lingering silence of the ruins and shivered. We found ourselves in a small courtyard flanked by what used to be small villas styled like the Romans used to build.

"Who lived here, I wonder?" I asked.

"Naturals," Elijah replied, pleased with his cleverness.

"*Duh.*"

We sat on the remains of a stone bench, the upper city towering over us. The Bobs hung back, giving us some privacy, though their gazes never left us.

"You seem…lucid today," I observed.

"It's that doctor's electrodes," Elijah explained. "They zapped some sense into me, but I can already feel it wearing off."

"Stunned the demon, did they?"

"I'm all twisted up inside," he remarked. "Two creatures in the one body. There's me and some genetically-modified virus-like entity. You know, I never knew that."

"Well, we're all a little twisted."

"I feel like I've got tapeworms."

I pretend to vomit and punched him on the arm. "Too much information."

"I know what I have to do," he said. "Your doctor told me before my playdate with that Thompson guy."

"But?"

He lowered his gaze and picked at the grass. "I've been hiding from it for a long time."

"You came to me for a cure—"

"I know."

"Will you at least try?"

"The future is unwritten, but the past holds all the secrets," he said, avoiding an answer entirely by spouting philosophical nonsense.

"Sounds like something a Druid would say."

He smiled and looked towards Camelot's inner castle. From here, we could see the very tops of the ruined towers etched against the sky.

"Ramona seems to think I'm part Druid," I confided softly.

Elijah looked at me, his expression unreadable. "I once heard rumours about the Dark using a Druidess in their experiments. They took her essence and she became a wraith of sorts." He shrugged. "I don't know if there was any truth to it."

"The Grey Lady," I murmured.

"The Grey who?"

"The Grey Lady," I replied. "She was supposedly a druidess who was holed up in some abandoned house in London collecting souls. The Dark had twisted her into something unrecognisable. She captured Wilder and tried to enslave him before he became Excalibur."

"Interesting," Elijah said. "Perhaps it's true, then."

"Well, Ramona compared my genetic markers to yours, and they match some unknown ones from your human side."

He made a face and shivered. "Does that mean we're brother and sister? Because that would shatter a lot of my hopes and dreams."

"I can see the effects of your electrocution has worn off."

"That Issac guy really has it out for me," he declared, veering the conversation in a one-eighty. "He's a massive arsehole."

"Takes one to know one," I retorted.

He laughed, slipping into clarity again. "Do you remember the cottage I took you to?"

"The one near the village?"

He nodded. "The pace where you kissed me."

I flushed and nestled against him. "What about it?"

"I wasn't able to go back and I left something there..." he cleared his throat, "something important."

Curiosity tugged at my heartstrings and I hoped he was about to trust me enough to attempt his cure. "What is it?"

"You'll know it when you see it."

I blew through my lips. "Way to be vague."

"It's important to who I was, and the Naturals won't let me leave."

Clearly, I was the only person he could ask, but it was my turn to be cunning. Elijah was getting his cure.

"If I get it for you, will you fight back against your Darkness?"

He looked up towards the ruined castle and sighed. "And face my past? And all the horrible things I've done since I lost myself? Death seems like a safer option."

I threaded my arm through his. "I will be with you the entire time."

Elijah leaned down and pressed his lips against my forehead. He lingered a moment and inhaled. Then he gave his answer. "Yes," he promised, "I will."

18

Once the sun had set, I slipped out of Camelot without stirring a soul.

I'd be there and back before anyone noticed I was gone, and if retrieving one of Elijah's lost secrets would help him regain his lost past, then the risk was worth it.

The old crofter's cottage was exactly how we'd left it weeks before. The small, dark stone building looked abandoned with ivy tangling around the single chimney and one whole side of the house.

I walked up the uneven path, my senses aware of things that lingered. Nothing stirred other than the reverberations of the wards and now that I understood what Elijah had been, I began to understand the power which covered this place. It was Druidic energy.

What I didn't understand was how he'd woven the illusion if he couldn't reach his Colours… unless this place had been built over a much older site inhabited by his people. I'd heard stories about places that held lingering power. Perhaps this was one of them?

Inside, the cottage was bare of any personal effects, and I wondered what Elijah had left behind and how he wanted me to find it. I walked around the small living space, trailing my fingers over the windowsill and the mantle over the open fireplace.

The bed was still unmade, the sheets stained with dried blood from the wounds that had almost taken Elijah's life. Longing tore at my heart and I turned away, remembering our first kiss, and the hope we could be together, free from Light and Dark. It hadn't worked out that way, though. He'd been ready to die that night, but instead, I'd taken him to Camelot.

I closed my eyes and pushed the memory aside, focusing on the surrounding cottage. He'd sent me to get something special. Something I'd know when I found it, which meant it had some kind of arcane connotations around it.

I was drawn towards the fireplace, so I opened my eyes and stood before it. People always hid things up chimneys and it mystified me as to why. It was the first place thieves looked, along with the hopes people had gaffer-taped stuff to the underside of drawers and other assorted furniture.

I reached into the cold fireplace and up the stack, feeling across the soot-covered bricks. My fingertips found a small ledge and a wrapped package fell into the ashes in the hearth. It was small, slightly larger than a pen, and tightly bound in grubby canvas material.

My palm began to tingle when I picked it up. Whatever it was, it held some kind of energy. I debated unwrapping it—maybe Elijah would be offended if I snooped—but curiosity got the better of me. It always did.

I unwound the little package, revealing a curious item within. As well as being a similar size, it also looked like a fancy, silver fountain pen. A clear quartz crystal was set in one end and the other clicked open to reveal a small, but razor-sharp, silver blade. The length was detailed with tiny runes, the inset markings dark with use and age.

I wasn't sure what it did, but I could feel echoes of power lingering inside the crystal and the intricate runes along the length.

Definitely Druid shenanigans.

I pocketed the knife and left the cottage behind, the little house disappearing into the landscape as the wards hid it from the outside world once more.

With my suped-up speed, I was back in Camelot in record time. I slipped through the barrier, eager to return to Elijah.

A loud cough made me freeze and I turned to find Maisy pouting like a disappointed parent who'd just caught their kid sneaking in after curfew. She pushed off the wall and stepped towards me, Light and shadow playing across her features.

"Really?" She sighed and nodded towards the barrier.

"I had to get something." The little crystal knife weighed heavily in my pocket. "For Elijah."

"You're not losing it over him again, are you?" she asked. "Because that would be a little silly, don't you think?"

"No," I replied with a sigh. "I'm not *going silly.*"

"Then I'll walk you back to Elijah's tent and we'll check."

"You don't have to do that."

"It wasn't that long ago you were having sex dreams about him," she declared.

My face heated up to inferno levels. "Fine. Let's go."

Maisy laughed as we walked through base camp. "You're too easy, Madeleine."

"Stop pressing my buttons," I complained. "You know I'm stupidly naïve about these things."

"Then don't rise to the occasion."

We gasped in unison as we pushed inside the tent. Smith and Thatcher were lying on the ground, completely out to it, and Elijah was gone.

He was gone.

"Oh, this is bad," Maisy declared as we stared down at the Bobs.

"*Elijah,*" I hissed under my breath as I checked for a pulse in Smith's neck. I didn't have to—I could feel his heart beating from where I stood—but I needed something to occupy myself while my mind reeled.

"He's unconscious," I said. "Maybe for a few minutes."

"That means he's still in the city," Maisy said. "Madeleine, we have to raise the alarm."

I ignored her and closed my eyes, searching

Camelot for signs of Elijah. He couldn't have passed through the barrier on his own without setting off the alarms, so he had to be somewhere in the city.

I didn't need to feel his presence to realise where he'd gone—the archive.

"*Madeleine*," Maisy snapped.

"Give me a five-minute head start," I pleaded. "I can talk him down with no one else getting hurt."

Her jaw tensed and she nodded. "Then you better run."

"Thank you."

I rushed out of the tent only to find Rhys waiting for me. In all the excitement and chaos of the past few weeks, I'd forgotten about him entirely.

"Well, if it isn't the demon lover," he drawled, curling his lip.

I sighed sharply as he blocked my path.

"Who saved your life, FYI," I retorted.

"You may have the others fooled, but I see right through you, Madeleine. Right into your black heart."

"I so don't have time for this." I slapped my palm against his forehead. My power zapped into his brain and his eyes rolled as he slumped to the ground, right into a muddy puddle.

I sprinted through base camp and as I rounded the corner into the lower city, I almost slammed into Trent. He cursed loudly and threw his hands into the air.

"Hey, slow down," he bellowed as I dashed past. "Where's the fire?"

His joke slid right off my back as I legged it up the

main thoroughfare towards the archive. It was late, so I was the only fool in the city.

Elijah had tricked me. He'd sent me on an errand to get me out of Camelot so he could do what? Leave?

When I burst into the foyer, I expected to find him at the portal but he was nowhere to seen. Where was…

The vault.

It all made sense now. The strange energy leaking through the doors, Wilder and Scarlett's coma, the way Ikakantor made the Naturals dig up the archive, the attack on Camelot, Masters' slow decent into madness, Elijah returning through the portal… It was all an attempt to get into the vault.

But they couldn't open the door without a Natural or Druid to do it for them. They couldn't corrupt me, but they'd gotten to Elijah. He'd given up his last shred of humanity and had given the Dark complete control.

This was the Dark's plan all along.

I thundered down the stairs, my power flaring as the energy that leaked from the vault oozed into my veins. The nausea almost made me stumble, but my mutation fought against it, the different facets of what I'd become bouncing around until the corrosive force was merely a dull throb in the back of my mind.

I reached the bottom of the stairs and stilled. A human form stood silhouetted in front of the metallic doors, outlined by the glow of Masters' golden Light barrier.

"Elijah, *stop*."

He turned, his black gaze meeting mine.

I glanced at Masters' prone body on the ground. Someone had overturned his table and his notes littered the hallway.

"Don't do this," I murmured, approaching with careful, considered steps. "This isn't you."

"You're right," he replied, his voice grating, "this isn't Elijah."

It wasn't a mutation. Elijah was *possessed*.

I could see it radiating inside him clear as day—a red vine of Darkness curled around his spine, its barbs stabbing into his brainstem. The essence was so ingrained inside his body, I couldn't tell where it began or where it ended.

Understanding was a strange thing when you suddenly realised you could call on the fire of the Earth itself. I felt it tug at me even as the power from the vault leeched onto me like a parasitic virus.

I wasn't looking at an Infernal demon, or a genetically-modified mutation implanted inside him. This thing was something much worse.

It was a shard of Ikakantor himself—the ultimate possession.

"Do not open that door," I urged. "You'll kill us all."

"My life doesn't matter. It hasn't been mine for a long time."

I understood so clearly, I began to shake with fury. When Elijah had been taken from his people eight hundred years ago, the greater demon must have placed a seed of his essence into the young Druid. Left unchecked, it had grown into its own entity that had strangled the magic and humanity out of him—he'd become a hybrid creature fuelled by Darkness.

Irrevocably linked to Ikakantor, he was powerless to resist the greater demon's compulsion until I'd come along and attempted to break it. Somehow, my presence had allowed his true self to bleed through. He'd seen clearly for the first time in centuries and sought me out in hopes for a cure. Now here we were.

Ramona and Issac were wrong about him, but how could they know? Not even Elijah understood what the Dark had turned him into.

The Druids were prized beings to the Dark. They'd been hunted to the brink of extinction, but to capture one? The implications were so great, I couldn't fathom what it had meant for the destruction of his people.

Elijah turned back to the vault and raised his hand.

"*Don't,*" I hissed.

"The Dark will rise," he rasped, taking a step towards the vault. "It's inevitable."

"*Not on my watch.*" I lunged, grasping his head in my hands, and plunged into his mind like a shard of cold iron.

The vault disappeared and I was standing inside a swirling mass of inky clouds, bolts of crimson electricity arcing towards me. I hissed, lashing out at Ikakantor's essence.

Elijah let out a strangled wail and clawed at my hands. "*Stop!*"

"You're not mutated, Elijah," I shouted through the fog. "*You're possessed.*"

Electricity zapped, lashing out in an attempt to push me out of his head. I pushed aside the Darkness inside me and called on the Light—and alleged Colour—and forced it into the essence clogging Elijah's mind.

I gasped as I was wrenched back into reality, forced out by my own pulse of energy.

"I didn't know," Elijah wailed, falling to his knees. "*I didn't know.*"

He was coherent for the time being, but I knew Ikakantor would try again.

I cupped his face in my hands and wiped at his tears. "This ends now."

"It's too late. *It's too late…*"

Ramona said the mutation had to be cut out at the root, but it would only work if Elijah wanted to face his past. There was no time left to wait for him to be ready. It was now or never.

"Elijah, listen to me…" I grasped his face and forced him to look into my eyes. "I understand how to free you, but you have to meet me halfway, okay?"

"I can feel him digging into my mind," he sobbed, the pain of eight hundred years of possession hitting him all at once.

"You have to face your pain and your past, otherwise this won't work."

"How can I? I've done so many things… I can't find redemption, Madeleine. I'm past saving."

"You're not. I saw your truth, Elijah. There's always hope."

"What if… What if I can't?"

"I'll be with you," I murmured. "Every step of the way."

He nodded and I knelt before him. "If I—"

"You're coming back with me," I promised. "No matter what."

"Then let it end how it will."

He drew me into his mind and I merged seamlessly with his subconscious. One moment I was kneeling before him in the archive, the next, I was standing in a foreign landscape of trees and moss-covered rocks. It wasn't a rainforest, but it was as dense and isolated as the one he'd taken me to in Borneo.

This forest was clogged with a dense greyish-black fog instead of humidity. It wrapped around the trees and settled in every available dip in the landscape like thick sludge.

I picked my way through the confusion inside Elijah's mind, searching out the place where Ikakantor had taken root.

The fog rippled to my left and I turned, seeking out the source. Something was out there, but I didn't know who I was about to encounter. Were they calling me?

I moved towards the source of the disturbance and flexed my fingers. I had to be ready for anything, but I wasn't expecting the reality of what I stumbled across.

A small boy was curled up in the hollow of an ancient willow. If it wasn't for my familiarity with his being, I would have passed right by him. His shaggy brown hair had snarled into a mess of dreadlocks and burrs, and his tunic and trousers were stained and torn.

"Elijah?"

He looked up at me, tears staining his grubby cheeks. His mind had curled in on itself, reverting him to a state where he felt small and safe inside his nightmare. No more than five years old, he was vulnerable and terrified.

I knelt beside him, my heart aching. "Why are you hiding?"

"*Shh*." He pressed his finger to his lips. "You'll wake the monster." He must mean Ikakantor.

"I'm not afraid of any monster," I told him. "I've come to slay him."

Elijah stared up at me in awe with his big emerald-coloured eyes.

"There's nothing to fear," I said, holding out my hand. "I've come to take you home."

He looked at my hand and shook his head.

"I've come to take you back to Camelot," I urged. "*Home*."

"Camelot?"

"Yes."

He scurried back against the tree. "The monsters ate everyone in Camelot. They ate my friends until they were bones."

I hesitated, realising why he didn't want to return. He'd said it hurt because he'd been there the day the rift opened. He'd been at the cataclysm and witnessed horror beyond imagining.

"*Oh, Elijah.*"

"They didn't eat us."

"You escaped?" I asked.

"We went to the forest and waited for Merlin," he told me. "But he never came."

"Merlin?"

He nodded vigorously. "They took everyone," he added. "We were supposed to go through the portal, but the monster came and stopped us."

"I'm sorry," I murmured.

"The monster didn't eat me."

"No, he didn't." I looked around the forest, but nothing else stirred. "Where did your people go?"

The boy shrugged. "They left me here alone. I found them before they went through the portal and they called me a monster and said I couldn't go." He narrowed his eyes, some of his boyish looks melting.

I sucked in a sharp breath, my heart breaking for the little boy trapped inside Elijah's mind. The Druids had left our world and turned their backs on him—his own people had exiled him rather than help.

Well, I wasn't going to let him suffer anymore.

"I'll never leave you," I murmured, holding out my hand. "Will you help me slay the monster once and for all?"

He thrust his grubby hand into mine and allowed me to haul his little body out of the hollow.

"Very good," I said with a smile. "Do you know where we can find the monster?"

He nodded enthusiastically and pointed behind me. I glanced over my shoulder and stilled when I saw a shadowy figure looming through the forest.

"I believe in you, Elijah," I said, ignoring the shade. "You need to reach really hard and find your Colours, okay? I'll use mine, too."

His grip tightened on my hand and I stood. Together, we turned and faced the shard of Ikakantor.

Cut it out at the root... I didn't have a sword, but fire would do just as well.

I called on my power, all three colours, and Elijah added his prism. The clearing began to glow with holographic shards, forcing the black sludge to retreat towards the shadow figure.

Elijah had once called me a spectre, but that wasn't entirely true. Ikakantor was the shade, and we were the Light. We'd declared for life in reality, and now we'd proclaimed it in the deepest way possible.

The Dark could fight to their dying breath, but we'd never give up who we were or what we believed in.

The glow intensified until it covered everything, blinding my eyes to Ikakantor and his parasitic hold on Elijah's soul. It purified, forcing Darkness out and Light into forgotten places.

My eyes began to water and I closed them, images playing across the backs on my eyelids. When I finally opened them, the forest remained and the shadows were gone.

Overhead, the sun was shining.

Warmth spread through my hand and I looked down to see coloured lines crawling over my wrist. Elijah smiled and they twisted and turned, weaving a complex path over my flesh. The geometric pattern grew, snaking up my arm to my elbow, flaring blue before it sank into my skin and became a part of me.

"You *are* a Druid," I whispered, looking up at the Elijah I knew.

He was free.

I could see the echoes of the boyish face I'd called through the fog, but I preferred the grown-up version. This one I could kiss.

"Was I that transparent?" he asked.

"No." I shook my head. "But eight hundred years? *Elijah.*"

"All that time living and I'm still as dumb as a bag of rocks."

"You were trapped."

"And so were you," he told me.

Footsteps echoed at the end of the hall as the cavalry arrived, the sound drawing us back into reality. The shadows cast by the barrier around the vault dimmed as we embraced for the first time.

Triune and Druid.

19

I lingered outside the infirmary, carving a dent into the soft earth. After delving into Elijah's mind, I was restless.

I'd always preferred the night. The mystery of the stars, the shadows I could hide in, and the subdued bustle of the city, but out here in Camelot, everything was intensified. I thought about Elijah and his forest, wondering why the willow tree was so special. I knew nothing about nature.

The door opened and Greer appeared. "Madeleine, what are you doing out here?"

"Pacing," I replied.

She watched me complete a few laps before she placed a hand on my shoulder.

"Why now?" I wondered. "After eight hundred years of occupation, why do they want to open the vault now when they had all that time?"

"They lost the rift and their connection to the One," she replied. "They need power to survive and they must believe it's held in the vault. It seems like it's potent enough to send Wilder and Scarlett into a coma. That's an asset worth attacking a fully garrisoned Camelot for, don't you think?"

I nodded. If the Flames couldn't stand against it, then what hope did the rest of us have?

"Come," she urged. "It's freezing out here and Elijah's waiting for you."

"Masters?"

"There's an impressive lump on his head, but he'll be fine."

I shivered and began to pace again.

"Are you feeling okay?" Greer asked.

"I'm restless. I guess… I guess I'm worried about Ikakantor. We cut him out of Elijah, but…"

Greer urged me forwards. "Come inside. We'll talk about it. Something has to be done, but we must make plans."

"No more winging it?"

"You have an uncanny knack for it, but we should think things through this time."

The infirmary was warm as Greer led me inside, but the temperature was frosty.

Elijah wasn't looking impressed with his situation when I set eyes on him. Ramona had given him a check-up, but he'd been left to deal with Issac. Considering he'd called the Natural various creative names in the last week, I wasn't surprised they were an inch from having another punch up.

Ramona was with Masters in a private room at the back, leaving us to talk without disturbing the

Light Studies professor. Good thing too, because tempers—mostly Issac's—were fraying.

"So, we're supposed to give him a pardon, no questions asked?" Issac glared at me, his dislike of Elijah clearer than it had ever been.

No hello, how are you. Straight to the insults. Issac was reminding me of his charming attitude at the Regula hearing in London.

"Yes," I stated. "He was possessed and was not in control of his actions."

"You don't have to protect me, Madeleine," Elijah murmured.

I looked up at him and shook my head. "I made you a promise and I will keep it." I turned to Greer and Issac. "You can see for yourself. His Darkness and Ikakantor's essence are both gone." I slid my hand into Elijah's. "He's cured."

"She's right, but I can't feel my Colours," he said. "I don't know if they will come back or if… I'm human."

"Ramona confirmed it, Issac," Greer said. "Elijah has no reason to wish us harm, nor is he compromised."

"I like her," the Druid whispered into my ear, sending a shiver down my spine.

Druid. Knowing made me all tingly inside, but also angry as a bee in a jar for what he'd been through—not only at the hands of the Dark, but also his own people. That was something we both had in common.

"Ikakantor has to die his true death," I snarled. "No matter the cost."

Issac grunted. "Those are strong words."

"He's not strong enough to get into Camelot without Elijah," I said. "We have to take the fight to him."

"He has no Darkness," Issac argued. "Ikakantor will know the moment he sets eyes on him and you'll both be dead."

"Not if I give him a little of mine," I declared.

"You can't be serious!"

"Just a little," I said, looking at Elijah. "Enough to get us both inside and my knife to his throat. By the time he realises the ruse, he'll already be a ball of flame."

"He will already know he's lost control of me," Elijah told me. "But he'll be weaker because of it."

"Then I don't see how this will work," Issac stated. "It's a fool's errand."

"I'm the only one who can get in and stand against him," I said.

"How are you going to kill him?" Greer asked. "What makes you sure you can end a greater demon?"

"Until now, you haven't been able to make a dent like the rest of us," Issac added. "If you're not certain, we can't risk losing you."

I shook my head. "No risk, no reward."

"Madeleine was able to destroy Ikakantor's presence inside me," Elijah said. His voice was calm and even, the tone making everyone fall into silence. This wasn't the same man who came through the portal ranting and raving. "It was a piece of his essence. His demonic soul. I believe she can do it."

"What if he uses your true name?" Issac argued. "Elijah can't help you without his powers."

"Everyone keeps telling me to isolate that part of myself and lock it away," I said. "I'm going to accept it and get on with killing that bastard."

"But—"

"*I am not Eilhana.*"

"It's called dilution," Elijah told him. "Look it up in a dictionary, pretty boy."

"Good to see he's lost none of his flare," Greer remarked.

"He had power over me because I believed he did," I continued. "It's difficult to explain…"

"I understand," Issac said. "Belief is a powerful notion."

I looked to Greer. "I'm going, but I'd like your blessing. I'd rather not break another direct order."

"I can see there's no reasoning with you," she replied. "You're our greatest hope, Madeleine. Without the Flames, we have nothing to protect this world from whatever lurks in the vault. Not until you rose."

"Which is why Ikakantor must be dealt with," I told her. "He'll keep coming until he gets what he wants, and no more people should have to die because of it."

"Good," Issac declared, crossing his arms over his chest. "I was beginning to think this was a revenge mission."

"Maybe a little," Elijah said. "I do have eight hundred years of carnage to avenge."

I elbowed him in the side and he chuckled softly. "Where would he be?"

"Ben Nevis," he replied.

"But we scoured the mountain after Madeleine returned from her capture," Greer said. "There was nothing there save for a few empty caves. Wilder went himself. If it was cloaked, he would have seen right through it."

"Impossible," I said with a shake of my head. "I saw the tunnels myself. They were like smooth obsidian and full of carvings. It was an intelligent settlement."

"It's there," Elijah murmured. "I can take you to it."

"We'll leave immediately," Issac said. "The fewer of us, the better."

"That's why only Elijah and I will go," I stated.

"But—"

"The moment Ikakantor dies, an entire mountain full of demons will come down on us," Elijah interrupted. "Madeleine and I must go, but any other lives will be at risk. The Naturals have already suffered too much because of my involvement."

"Elijah," I hissed. "None of this was your fault."

"Still, it's my duty to fix it." He cupped my face in his hand, the intimate touch causing my face to heat. "Besides, you'll be there."

Issac coughed loudly and when I pulled away from Elijah, I looked up to find him glaring at us. If there was any question left unanswered about feelings, I'd just allowed Elijah to declare for me.

"It seems like it's a risk we have to take," Greer said, watching us with her wise, unearthly gaze. "The Codex and the Regula stand with you both."

"It's an eight-hour drive," Elijah told the assembled Naturals. "We must leave immediately."

"We can prepare a vehicle," Issac said, "and weapons."

Greer nodded. "Elijah, before you leave, I want to have a word."

I looked to him and he nodded. "Go. Get what we'll need and I'll meet you outside."

Leaving him behind with Greer, Issac and I parted ways outside. While he went to get a pickup truck, I ransacked the weapons tent, finding another arondight blade and an assortment of cold iron daggers.

Demons barely registered any pain when regular blades cut them open, but the metal forged from meteorites had them screaming like little babies. Stab one with one of these with a well-aimed jab and they were bursting into flame before they realised they were dead.

I flipped each dagger over in my hand, checking the balance between hilt and tip, before selecting the four best. I grabbed Elijah a new jacket and belt and gave the room a quick scan to make sure I'd selected everything we'd need.

Outside, I found the pickup truck parked and

waiting. I was lining up everything in the tray when Issac appeared beside me.

"Have you got everything you need?"

"I think so," I replied. "There's not much to take."

"Snacks?"

I looked up at him and laughed. "Well, maybe we could pack a few bags of crisps."

"It's nice to see you smile. Things have been way too serious around here."

"Well, we haven't spoken much since…" I trailed off awkwardly.

"Our jungle adventure?" He snorted. "That's an overnighter I'd like to forget."

"At least we didn't get eaten by snake people."

"Do you love him?" he asked straight up, taking me by surprise.

"I don't know what I feel for him," I admitted. "It's likely that I love him, but I'm not sure I understand what kind of love it is."

I'd walked inside Elijah's mind and made promises I'd die to keep. I fought for him with the conviction of a lover. He'd reached out to me when all others had turned their backs. We'd stood together against his darkest fears. We'd kissed like we were meant to be.

But was it the real thing or merely a fantasy? I wanted it to be the forever kind of real, but that was a conversation I needed to have with Elijah.

"Well," Issac said. "How can I compete with a Druid?"

"I respect you, Issac. You looked past your

prejudice and helped me when I needed it the most. I don't think I could have controlled that fire without your lessons." I looked across the camp where Elijah and Greer had emerged from the infirmary. "We shared things that we'd never shared with one another, and I will always feel humbled that you chose me to tell them to. I've never had that in my life before."

He nodded. "Trust is a fragile thing."

"And I'd never betray yours." I resisted the urge to take his hand. "I don't want to lose you, Issac."

He looked across the camp and I knew he'd seen Elijah approach. He grimaced and ran his hand over the cold iron daggers, his thoughts unknown. It can't be easy, knowing someone he cared about was into someone else.

After a moment, he said, "I'll always be here."

"And so will I."

He smiled and grasped my shoulder. "Good luck. To the both of you." The last sentence seemed a little reluctant, but I took it anyway.

"Thank you."

I watched after him as he moved away to talk to the guards by the wall, his departure perfectly timed to avoid Elijah, who joined me at the back of the pickup truck.

"What did he want?"

I followed Elijah's gaze to Issac, who was handing out orders to the guards.

I shrugged. "We had a few things to work out."

"Like?" His glare intensified and I saw the jealousy behind it.

"Not you, too." I sighed and shook my head in frustration. "What are we, Elijah? We're about to go face a powerful greater demon and I'm not sure which of my problems worries me the most."

He blinked. "I'm a problem?"

"I can fight demons and raise lava from the Earth's core, but relationships? That's my greatest struggle. Not true names or battling demons inside your mind, but…" I pursed my lips. I couldn't even say it, though I'd admitted as much to Issac only moments ago. *Oh, the irony.*

Elijah lifted my right arm and pushed up my sleeve, his fingers caressing my skin. "I'm connected to you."

I remembered the geometric pattern as I followed his movements. Drawing in a deep breath, I met his gaze. "But what does it mean?"

"Sometimes I forget how young you are," he murmured, "and how alone I am."

"Your people abandoned you. I won't, but—"

"You're afraid to let anyone else hold your heart." He rolled my sleeve back down. "I understand."

I shook my head. "The pattern?"

"That was me declaring for you," he told me.

"Declaring what?"

"My love."

They were two simple words, but they held a great deal of things I didn't understand. Maybe he was right. I was too young.

"C'mon," he said, his Scottish accent thickening, "time is short and the road is long."

I tugged on his arm. "Elijah?"

He paused.

"It's difficult for me," I admitted. "I've been bullied, ostracised, my family is indifferent… I've spent my whole life making myself small. I know isolation. I know secrets. Now it seems like I'm *larger* than I ought to be." I lowered my gaze. It was so not the time to be talking about these things, but there was no telling what awaited us at Ben Nevis. "I don't know how to live."

Elijah cupped my face, bringing my chin up. "You know more than you realise, pretty triune."

I swallowed the lump in my throat and smiled. "At least I know how to kick demon arse."

"That's a good start."

"I got you some things." I turned to the arondight hilt and cold iron daggers.

He raised an eyebrow and held up the hilt. "An arondight blade?"

"Your Druid blood will allow you to use it," I told him. "You could before, and there's no reason you shouldn't now." I picked up the belt and wrapped it around his waist and clipped the buckle in place. Finally, I slid the hilt into the holder and one dagger on the opposite hip.

"I like it when you dress me," Elijah murmured. "But even better the other way around."

"I can see you're experiencing echoes."

"I'm immune to those." His lips quirked and he picked up the jacket I'd gotten him. "Let's hit the road. We've got a demon to send back to Hell."

20

The drive to Ben Nevis was a quiet affair.

I had so many questions I wanted to ask Elijah, but I knew pushing him to relive his time at Camelot was a step too far. Especially when the fight of our lives was looming.

He'd offered to drive, so I watched him as he watched the road. There was no doubt he was different. His whole demeanour had changed, and I began to wonder what part of him I'd fallen for. Was Elijah a different person now that his demonic side had been removed?

"You're staring at me," he said, his hands tightening around the steering wheel.

"We didn't say goodbye to anyone."

"We don't have to," he replied. "We're going back."

"You sound so confident."

"It'll be over before you know it. In and out. Destruction takes but a second." He placed his hand on my thigh and squeezed. "One well-aimed strike and it's all over."

If I was doubting our relationship, he'd just dispelled my anxiety with one touch.

"So, I get us into the caves unseen, you distract Ikakantor, and I drive my knife into his proverbial heart."

"Best to keep it simple, don't you think?" he asked.

"Quick and silent."

Our conversation dulled as we coasted through the Scottish Highlands, the hills climbing into mountains. The landscape became rugged with jagged rocks, twisting streams, and lush greenery. Cloud and mist clung to the tops of the peaks, layering the vista with an air of unbridled romance.

"Scotland is beautiful," I said as the countryside rolled past my window.

"It's wild country for sure," Elijah murmured. "In my time, the Highland Clans ruled supreme, and Druids lived amongst the lonely landscape."

"Really?"

"I'm sure there's still places to be found where they once lived." His eyes became misty as he spoke about his memories. "The Druids built burial cairns on top of these peaks."

The road curved and treated us with our first views of Loch Linnhe. In the distance, the tip of Ben Nevis sat in low cloud cover, all hidden and mysterious. Snow clung to the highest crags, coating the entire chain of mountains. Ben Nevis was the tallest mountain in the UK, but still a baby compared to other parts of the world.

"Did they bury their dead up here so they could be closer to the sky?" I wondered.

"Yes."

I risked another question, hoping he'd answer it. "Did you live near here?"

"No." I guess that's what I got for not asking open-ended questions. "Merlin wandered these mountains, though. He frequented the trails of Ben Macdui so often, the locals thought the mountain was haunted. They called him the Grey Man of Macdui. *Am Fear Liath Mòr.*"

We crossed the bridge over Loch Linnhe, the pickup truck bumping over a pothole on the other side.

"Did you ever meet him?"

"I don't want to talk about that man," he said thinly.

Duly noted.

"You should speak Gaelic more often," I said to lighten the air now that we were in the mountain's shadow of doom. "With your accent, it's rather sexy."

"*Tha gaol agam ort-fhèin.*"

"Do I want to know what—" The words tore from my mouth as the pickup truck slammed into something hard, then the nose dipped to the road as the tray hurtled up and over.

Glass shattered as metal twisted and groaned as the pickup truck flipped, careening down the road. We went over and over, tumbling like two stones inside a washing machine. My head hit the passenger side window and snapped back the other way, leaving me dazed. I didn't know which way was up until we landed, the car coming to a rest on its roof.

My head spun as the clicking of the engine and the sound of freewheeling tyres reverberated through the cab.

Blinking, I swatted at the blood that was dripping into my eyes, the stench of burnt rubber and hot metal filling my nose. Through the shattered windscreen, I could see the road and beyond, a pair of boots walking towards us.

"Elijah," I hissed. "*Elijah.*"

He didn't reply. He was hanging upside down, still strapped into the driver's seat, completely out cold. Blood covered his face and his arms dangled uselessly.

I felt the Darkness pierce the ringing in my ears and wrenched at my seatbelt. The clasp clicked open and I fell, my shoulders hitting the crumpled roof.

The smell of rotting flesh began to drift through the windows as the demon approached and I knew if I didn't get out of here right now, we were both dead.

I dragged myself out of the wreckage, pain stinging through my entire body. I didn't know what hurt the worst, but as I moved, I began to heal. Elijah wasn't so lucky. He didn't have his powers anymore, so if I didn't get us out of this mess and get him to a hospital… I didn't even want to think about losing him.

I used my elbows to haul myself away from the wreckage and towards the approaching Darkness. I looked up at our attacker and didn't recognise the face, but there was no doubt in my mind who inhabited the rotting meat suit.

"Ikakantor."

He flinched slightly, but the name did nothing to dent his strength. "*Eilhana.*"

"Well. Like you," I glared up at him and pushed to my knees, "I've learned a few tricks of my own."

"Impressive, but it won't save you from death."

"I'm not interested in conversation, you piece of rotting shite. I'm here to kill you and I'm not leaving this road until you're a ball of flame."

"Such brave words." He laughed, the sound echoing across the lonely wilderness. "I cannot be killed. When this body expires, I will make another. And another. *And another.* I will get what I want, and Camelot will be the first place to burn."

I slipped my arondight blade from my belt and allowed the blade to erupt. The links clicked together, showering silver and red sparks across the asphalt. *One well-aimed strike.*

"Your Natural sword won't leave a scratch," Ikakantor drawled. "I'm disappointed in you, Eilhana."

"A sword is merely a tool," I murmured.

He took a step towards me. "We could have ruled this world together."

"Excuse me while I vomit."

"You stole my Druid and murdered my people."

When he put it like that, it sounded as if he had a valid argument, but demons weren't people. They were creatures who did nothing but consume and destroy before moving onto their next victim. This is what the Naturals fought to stop—the destruction of life itself.

"Demons lie," I snarled.

"But…isn't that what you are?"

I bristled. "I wouldn't make me angry, Ikakantor. You think you're invincible, but I cut you out of Elijah's mind without even breaking a sweat. You're so dead, I don't know why we're still standing here."

The greater demon snarled and launched himself at me, leaping through the air with a burst of Darkness.

I pirouetted, moving like lightning and striking with my arondight blade. The sword cut through the soft flesh of Ikakantor's stomach and I twisted as the contents of his gut spilled out onto the road.

I grasped him around the neck, my power hissing as it ate through his rotting flesh. *"I hope you rot in hell."*

I forced the full brunt of my power into his body, the flow of energy tugging at my mind. The world fell away and I was nothing but energy—the road, the twisted wreckage of the pickup truck, Elijah, and everything was gone.

I'd become my own brand of essence, transcending my physical body, consuming the parasitic spirit clutched in my hand. I expanded, humming with Light, Colour, and Darkness until it merged into one, and bore down on my enemy.

Ikakantor screamed as his body broke down under the pressure and his Dark essence burst into flames.

The fireball wrapped around my hand, the pain threatening to break my hold, but I didn't let go. I wouldn't back down until I was sure he'd suffered his true death.

He would torment us no more.

The twisting flames crackled with red sparks, the heat intensifying before it sucked in on itself…then disappeared completely.

I gasped, my hand searing as the blistered burn began to heal. The medicinal properties of being three different kinds of supernatural was paying off for once. I could get used to this.

"And that's how it's done." I spat at the stain of entrails on the road. "*Good riddance.*"

A crashing sound tore me out of my daze and I turned towards the wreck where Elijah was attempting to drag his broken body out of the pickup truck.

"Elijah!"

Snapping to attention, I ran down the road and I grasped his arms, helping him the rest of the way. He leaned against me as I set him on the grass by the side of the road. Grasping his face, I checked the gash on his forehead and to my astonishment, the torn flesh began to knit itself back together.

"Elijah… your Colours…"

"You killed him," he rasped. "You killed Ikakantor."

I wrapped my arms around his trembling body and held him close. "Told you so." He groaned and I pulled back. "Are you healing?"

"I think so," he whispered as he screwed up his face. He fisted his hands into the grass and took a deep breath. He shivered, his teeth chattering.

"We can wait here for a moment." I shucked off my jacket and draped it around his shoulders.

"I'm supposed to do that," he told me. "It's not very chivalrous of me."

Remembering I'd forgotten about his crystal knife, I took it out of the inside pocket and handed it to him. "Here. Will this help?"

"My iPencil!" he declared with a theatrical gasp, obviously feeling better already. "I thought I'd be stuck using my finger on my iPad for all eternity."

"*Hysterical*," I drawled, sitting beside him. "What is it, exactly?"

"It's a nwyfre stele, but we always just called them nwyfre." It was a strange word, *noo-iv-ruh* and he etched the word into the dirt.

"That sounds nothing like it's spelt." I wondered if it was Welsh in origin.

"I know. It's vexing." He showed me the stele. "The crystal harnesses energy and the knife is for ritualistic bloodletting."

I raised my eyebrows, doubting him until I realised he was telling the truth. "Bloodletting?"

"Inexperience requires insurance," he said. "Blood seals where skill cannot."

"Seems a little...painful."

"All children have one," he told me. "Though they're mostly useless by adulthood."

"You let children cut themselves?"

He clucked his tongue. "It's so the Colours know you're serious. Adolescent brains aren't developed enough to consolidate the intent behind a prism."

I shook my head. "I don't think I'll ever understand half the things you say."

"Druidic magic is complicated."

"Do you think they'll come back entirely?" I asked. "Your Colours?"

"I don't know," he murmured. "But I'm free. After centuries of turmoil, it's…peaceful."

"At least there's enough to heal you. Are you feeling better?"

"Some." Elijah smiled and looked to the summit of Ben Nevis. "There's enough to get me back on feet, but after…"

"It's gone again, hasn't it?"

He lowered his gaze and clutched the stele against his chest. "We should move from here. More demons will come."

"Can you walk?"

"Yes."

I helped him to his feet and glanced at the wrecked pickup truck on the road. "What now?"

"The Dark will be scattered without someone to lead them," Elijah replied. "They may not recover. We need to take advantage and help your friends wake from their coma."

"I was wondering how we were going to get back to Camelot, but that works, too."

He smirked and nodded down the road. "There was a village not far that way."

"Well," I murmured, "let's go home."

Home. Camelot. The place that had been the site of so much of his suffering. Would he come now that Ikakantor was dead and he was free? I wouldn't blame him if he wanted to go back to the rainforest in Borneo.

"Yes," Elijah replied, pulling me in for a kiss, "let's go home."

21

Deep below Camelot, the earth stirred.

Outside the silver and brass door, the little man worked diligently on his magical creation, pouring his very being into his web. Light trickled through the gaps of the mechanical lock, bringing air and colour to an otherwise dark space.

How long had it been? A millennia? Time had lost all meaning, but it didn't matter.

The little man, in his ignorant stupidity, had come to open Camelot's very own Pandora's box. His mind had unravelled and his creation had almost eroded the lock.

Almost…

Ever so quietly, in the darkness of Camelot's forgotten past, the smallest cog began to turn.

OTHER BOOKS IN THE CAMELOT ARCHIVE

by Nicole R. Taylor

Demon Bound #1
Demon Sworn #2
Demon Forged #3
Demon Eternal #4

Go back to where it all began:
THE ARONDIGHT CODEX

An ancient war with demons. A lost sword with the power to end it all. And a woman with purple hair is the world's only hope.

Dark Descent #1
Dark Illusion #2
Dark Abandon #3
Dark Genesis #4
Dark Crucible #5

ABOUT NICOLE

Nicole R. Taylor is an Australian Urban Fantasy author.

She lives in the western suburbs of Melbourne dreaming up nail biting stories featuring sassy witches, duplicitous vampires, hunky shapeshifters, and devious monsters.

She likes chocolate, cat memes, and video games.

When she's not writing, she likes to think of what she's writing next.

Follow Nicole Online:

Website: www.nicolertaylorwrites.com
Facebook: facebook.com/nrtaylorwrites
Newsletter: www.nicolertaylorwrites.com/newsletter
Email: nicole.this.is@gmail.com

DEMON FORGED (THE CAMELOT ARCHIVE - BOOK THREE)

A SNEAK PEEK…

CHAPTER ONE

The sun rose over Camelot, bathing the ruined city in the fire of a new day.

It was unseasonably warm—just last week we'd been expecting snow—though I wasn't complaining. The growing light made the crumbled buildings look mysterious and romantic.

I sat atop a wall in the upper city—otherwise known as the posh part of town—and looked over the inner castle. Once it had been the palace that housed the great Natural king, Arthur Pendragon and his queen, Guinevere…until it was ripped apart and demons flooded into the world.

I wondered what they'd make of us now. Wilder, the last living descendant of the Pendragon bloodline, was the Natural embodiment of Excalibur, just like Scarlett Ravenwood was Arondight—the swords gifted by the Lady of the Lake and tore the world in two.

And me… I wondered what they'd think of Madeleine Greenbriar and the things she'd done to save Camelot.

I was a Triune—part Natural, part demon, part Druid. It was a lot to take in, but at least it had a name of sorts.

I couldn't believe that my powers were still evolving, bringing with it the fear of losing control. I'd already done so many impossible things—like calling forth molten lava from the earth, altered people's memories, freed Elijah from his possession, and killed a greater demon—and the thought of more was overwhelming.

"How did I know I'd find you here?"

I looked down at the sound of Elijah's voice and smiled at the sight of him. He was so handsome it hurt, and when he looked at me like he was right now… Shivers. Inappropriate ones.

It had been two weeks since Elijah and I had gone to Ben Nevis to confront Ikakantor. We hadn't quite made it, though. The greater demon had met us on the road and flipped our car, totalling it with us inside. Thankfully, Elijah had enough Druidic magic left to heal himself, otherwise… Well, I wouldn't know what to do if I'd lost him.

His hair had grown out a little since he'd returned to Camelot from his rainforest hideout. He usually kept it shaved all over, but I liked the length—it made him look even more roguish than usual.

He looked up at me with his ethereal green eyes and raised his eyebrows. "Everything okay?"

"Yeah," I replied. "I'm just thinking."

"About me, I hope."

"You're hopeless," I groaned.

Elijah climbed up the wall and sat beside me. "Aren't you leaving for London today?"

I watched him swing his feet back and forth, the heels of his boots hitting the wall beneath us. "Yeah, in an hour or so."

Elijah was silent for a moment, then asked, "Are you worried?"

I shrugged. "The archive bothers me."

The archive sat below the upper city and was full of unknown knowledge and power of the Naturals. Things we'd thought we'd lost forever had begun to resurface but with a heavy price. The Dark had bewitched the Naturals to dig it up because at its depths lay a vault they'd do anything to open. They'd even tried to force their way inside Camelot to get to it…until I'd stopped them.

The vault. Everything was about what lay behind those enormous locked doors.

"The vault has been quiet," Elijah said. "You told me so yourself."

"I know, but—"

"Are you feeling sick again?" The leaking energy from it had made me nauseous, but it subsided after I'd killed Ikakantor—that's how I realised I was sensitive to Darkness in the first place.

I shook my head. "No, but that's not what I meant."

"Come here." Elijah tugged me against his side and stroked his hand through my long black hair. "Without Ikakantor trying to claw his way inside, the power has settled. We've got time to work it out, Madeleine."

I breathed in the leathery scent of his jacket. "What if something happens while we're gone?"

"You don't have to be responsible for *everything*. The Naturals have experts working on sealing the vault. Ramona believes that once it's taken care of, the Twin Flames will wake from their coma."

Masters—my old Light Studies professor from the academy—was the expert working on the barrier, but I worried about his mental state. He'd become obsessive about his work, remaining in the archive for days at a time, forgetting to eat and sleep. It was difficult not to worry about him.

"It's time for us to rest," Elijah added. "We've fought enough for now, don't you think?"

I smiled. "I am a little tired. Too bad Aiden sealed the portal. We could have gone to Barbados."

"It went to Tahiti, actually."

I rolled my eyes. "A tropical beach is a tropical beach."

We laughed, but Elijah's smile faded faster than mine.

"What is it?" I murmured.

"I've been working with Ramona to repair the damage done to my soul," he began, taking my hand in his. His fingers trailed across my knuckles, but he said nothing else.

"They haven't come back, have they?" I asked with a heavy heart. "Your Colours?"

"I was possessed by a shard of Ikakantor's soul for eight hundred years…there'll always be scars in my spirit."

"I don't understand," I murmured. "Your Colours manifested on that road. I saw it."

"What little power I had left depleted when my body healed itself after the crash."

I understood. His soul was too damaged for his power to remain. It lingered under the surface, but they'd lost their ability to charge.

"Elijah…"

"It is what it is," he said. "We can keep trying. At least I'm alive and not withering away before your eyes. I like to think I'm a handsome man, but a wrinkly husk isn't attractive, especially when my girlfriend is an eleven."

My heart leapt. "I'm your girlfriend?"

"Controversial, isn't it?" He wiggled his eyebrows. "The last Druid and the only Triune. You think we could have spread around the awesome at least a little. You know, widen the gene pool."

I slapped his arm. *"Smart arse."*

It seemed his time as a demon had shaped his personality and now that he was free, some echoes still lingered. Though he was stoic and quite thoughtful as a Druid, Elijah had a sharp sarcastic wit as a demon that I found annoying, yet rather attractive. I was kind of glad it had stuck around—his comedic timing was always on point.

"I may not have declared you as a Druid should, but it still counts." Until he turned serious again, that was.

"The pattern on my arm?" I asked, remembering the geometric shape that crawled up my right arm and sunk into my skin. "I was in your mind."

"Exactly. I should've done that while we were both conscious. Then when I touched you…" he slipped his palm under the sleeve of my jacket and pushed it upwards, "it would come to life." His fingers traced invisible lines. "A holographic declaration of love."

"Stop that," I said, beginning to squirm.

"Am I making you—"

"*Elijah.*"

His lips quirked. "You're beautiful when you flush."

"I'm… I'm not ready for that."

His expression changed, but he wasn't angry, which put me at ease. "Do you want to walk back to base camp?"

"Sure."

We jumped off the wall and landed softly onto the ground below. Elijah might not have his powers, but he was light on his feet and could hold himself in a fight. Some skills never went away, no matter what arcane abilities we had to back them up.

Base camp was alive with activity when we arrived. Tomorrow was the sixth-year anniversary of the Dark Night attacks and while the official proceedings happened in London, Camelot was having its own remembrance ceremony.

It seemed more important than ever to take the time to pay our respects to those who fell to the Dark on that terrible night.

In the weeks before the Twin Flames closed the rift, nine Sanctums had fallen in a coordinated attack led by the demon hybrid, Mordred—from whom my mutation originated—including London. The Naturals had been scattered, but in the aftermath of the war, we'd rebuilt and then some. Camelot had been returned to us.

As we approached, I spotted Greer and Issac talking beside the convoy of sleek black sedans. Issac still seemed to harbour some resentment towards Elijah over his convoluted past as a demon-hybrid, but he was doing a good job of hiding it. *Mostly.*

When they saw us approach, Issac broke away, leaving us alone with Greer. *Subtle.*

"Your bag has already been taken care of," she told me, seemingly oblivious to Issac's abrupt departure. Turning to Elijah, she smiled. "Though I'm told we don't have yours."

"You want me to come?" He seemed taken aback by the suggestion.

"If you're going to stay with us, then you will benefit from learning a few of our customs. We aren't the same Naturals you once knew."

"Come," I urged. "It will be good to have you there."

He looked uncomfortable being invited to

something that usually wasn't for outsiders, but he nodded. "Sure. Give me five minutes?"

Greer smiled and gestured towards camp. "Certainly. We'll wait for you."

I waited until he was out of earshot before I turned to the acting Inquisitor. "That was really nice of you."

"He has nowhere else to go," she replied sadly. "Camelot was once his home as much as it was ours. The Druids will forever be welcomed amongst the Naturals."

I grimaced. I wondered if she'd change her tune if she knew what they'd done to Elijah.

"Come," she said, oblivious to my internal deliberations. "You and Elijah can ride together. I'll share a car with Issac."

I laughed and nodded. Maybe she knew more about what was going on than I'd ever know.

***

Demon Forged is OUT NOW!